Ann Rutledge

**Ann Rutledge**

heart story of the early Lincoln

Ann Rutledge

**Ann Rutledge**
*heart story of the early Lincoln*

ISBN/EAN: 9783744736237

Printed in Europe, USA, Canada, Australia, Japan

Cover: Foto ©Raphael Reischuk / pixelio.de

More available books at **www.hansebooks.com**

# ANN RUTLEDGE

## HEART STORY OF THE EARLY LINCOLN

*With Frontispiece*

PHILADELPHIA, PA.

# INTRODUCTION

AREFUL biographers, dealing with the life of Abraham Lincoln, have had, almost without an exception, something to say with more or less of detail, on the subject of his early love for Ann Rutledge, the attractive young woman of good family, of the town of New Salem, Illinois, in which he also lived during the period of what may be termed the twilight time of his existence, embracing as it did the strenuous days of his struggle through the drudgery of an experience as a young country store-keeper and self-taught land-surveyor, to the inner gateway of the high and honorable calling which later brought him such celebrity. It was the formative period of his life in which enthusiasm over high hopes and aspirations alternated with spells of deep dejection, if not of despair, as he would contrast his condition of dire poverty with that of more fortunately-placed young men of his age whose craft of life seemed to sail forward smoothly before an ever-fair wind while his labored and, at times, almost foundered on the same waters, causing him many bitter hours of brooding and soul-wrestling alone in the secret recesses of his profound being. If he suffered greatly at times it was because he was possessed of a nature with a capacity for suffering, as well as with a yearning for the highest and most sacred of the joys of life,—a nature boundless as the universe in its conception of lofty and noble accomplishments in the world of men. When he saw things phenomenally strange in comparison with his native surroundings, as for example, a great city such as was New Orleans in his day, he saw more than others of his crude environment would see because he perceived with a larger, a more intelligent and discriminating vision. He had the seeing eye as well as the understanding mind, and, while he was practically unschooled, in the sense of institutional training, it is a safe proposition to offer that, had he visited the Crescent City in company with some other one who had been a college graduate, both seeing the Southern Babylon for the first time, he would have observed vastly more, noted the new sights with a larger sense of their significance and relationship, and brought away with him a prodigiously greater store of knowledge of the place and of imagery and ideas in connection with types of men and manners and customs of city people generally, than his companion could even dare hope to have acquired in the time afforded for the visit, even if he ever, on frequently recurring trips, found himself able to measure it, with the scope and accuracy in the matter of its ways and institutions, as the other would in a sojourn there of twenty-four hours.

The heart that could later thrill the breasts of millions, as in the Gettysburg address, had its deep moods and abstractions, originating and fostered in the loneliness of a sombre, unlighted childhood on the dim frontier, where the eager young being, despite its surroundings, was ever trying its wings in the cherished expectation of being able some day to soar into the bright heaven of its hopes and dreams. A youth possessed of such high ideality and aspirations, would necessarily love deeply when his affections took root, and it required no skilled analyst of human nature to make clear the fact that such a life had in store for it the grim suggestion of tragedy.

The suitor for the hand of Ann Rutledge was therefore not an ordinary person, even in his poverty and humble worldly condition, and, in view of his large earnest nature, it was not to be expected his passion would react on him with the same effect it would in the case of one of the average type, once he was deeply in love. Because of the rarer, richer depths of his sincerity and sympathies, and the world of devotion his idealistic being would bring to the cherished object, the engaging of the affections of his heart meant more to him than it would have signified to any other man who had succumbed to the charm of woman. The fact that after the great life had been closed by assassination, the President's devoted friend and law-partner for twenty years, William H. Herndon, proposed to undertake a lecture-tour and enlighten the public on the sorrow-shrouded part of the young Lincoln's history and the consequences of the loss of his intended mate upon him mentally, for a time, and that he gave a preliminary talk on the subject to a select body of friends in the old Court House at Springfield in November, 1866, which was so harrowing in its recital that he was persuaded to abandon the idea, is in itself impressive proof of the distress of mind into which he who was to be the Nation's leader during its most stressful period, was plunged by his bereavement. A book, afterward published by Mr. Herndon, in a limited edition, recounts many of the vagaries of the heart-broken and temporarily distraught lover, the matter related there being a portion of the Court House address mentioned. The quotation of some of the wild expressions he would utter reminds one strikingly of Hamlet at the grave of Ophelia and calls up the same state of feeling one experiences in reading this part of the story of the Prince of Denmark in Shakespeare's dark and moving tragedy.

The young merchant and law-student became engaged to Miss Rutledge when she was recovering from a distressing experience of the heart through the perfidy, as claimed, of a former lover, who had come to New Salem from the East and to whom she had been affianced, with the understanding that the marriage should take place on his return from a journey to his home in New York whence he was to bring his parents to make settlement in the new country. He failed to come back in the time promised and the waiting bride-to-be presently received information through some source that he was an impostor and had been passing under an assumed name.

Her inward sorrow over the affair did not detract from the loveliness of her features, her pensive brooding state rendering her even more attractive to the tall, idealistic young merchant, surveyor, law-student and man-of-all-work who had long loved her in his secret heart, and who now in her time of trouble felt a sympathy for her in addition to his affection, which vibrated from the depths of his being. How much his own heart had suffered in silence, in his diffidence and self-abnegation, since his love for the attractive young girl had grown from a spark to a flame, could be known only to himself. From little acts of kindness, he at length ventured the offer of more regular attentions which were well received, and finally he became a suitor and eventually won her consent, and they became engaged. Their pledge was made with the understanding that a year should elapse before they married, Lincoln's straightened circumstances at the time precluding the hope that he could maintain her in the position he would wish until his prospects brightened, and her parents, on their part, desiring that she should have another term at school before entering into matrimony.

She was sent away accompanied by her brother, David, to the town of Jacksonville to an Academy, the nearest institution of learning from New Salem, and there remained through the winter term of 1834-5. Her health, however, had begun to fail through brooding over the apparent falseness of her former lover, and the notoriety and gossip created by the story that she had been jilted, and when she returned home she was no longer the bright, vivacious girl they had formerly known. Her pale face, hollow cheeks and the unnatural brightness of her eyes alarmed her family and friends. The misgivings of young Lincoln over her altered appearances were, in a measure, offset by the hope he cherished that home-care and the change of habits incident to the quitting of her studies would bring a restoration of health, and he became more constant than ever in his attendance at the shrine of his divinity, the centre of his hopes and of his future happiness. Her intelligence, not less than her beauty, had early impressed him, and, in the conversations they enjoyed in their walks together, he found such heaven on earth as he, in his life of strenuous toil and struggle, had never known before. She was a lover of books, as was he himself, and her thirst for knowledge, as that in his own case, was unquenchable. Their situation in the new country on the far western frontier, remote from the older civilizations of the early colonies of the East, rendered their aspiring minds more keen for the opportunities of learning, which were so easily within the reach of their more fortunately-placed contemporaries; and, the reader may, without difficulty, comprehend with what yearnings their eager souls dwelt upon the far-separated polished lands, fringing the Atlantic Coast, in contrast with their own isolation. In their communings together and in the outgivings of their mutual sympathies and confidences they lived a sort of dream-life and conjured up from the Past with its glorious traditions, a wealth of splendid imagery connected with the heroic founders of the country and of the Nation, thus reacting from their own crude surroundings with their obvious limitations. It is with this dream-life period of the future Great President, the present work has to deal, and if it shall become apparent that there are depths of sentimental affection displayed in his attachment to the one he loved and lost, that were not suspected in the public character that stood with such grandeur later before the eyes of the world, it should be borne in mind that certain men of profound natures and high capabilities have within them, to an exceptional degree, the faculty of self-repression, and, once dedicated to a great cause, that which lies deep and sacred in the heart-recess is placed far beyond the sound of world-tumults in which its bearer may be called on to command and arbitrate, and thus exemplify, in the performance of the public duties and trusts imposed on him, the highest instance that can be reckoned of loyalty and self-sacrifice. While the plaudits of a Nation may ring in the ears of such a man and the upflinging of arms and the waving of emblems of enthusiasm and admiration may greet his eyes, there may lie a bleeding heart within him which no earthly palliative can solace or cure. With such natures the ordeal of a great sorrow may leave its traces on the countenance and in the look of the eyes, as indelibly as fire, or a knife-thrust, may leave its enduring cicatrix on the cheek.

It was not for any length of time young Lincoln and his intended bride enjoyed their delightful rambles. The dread Disease was upon her and the day came when she could no longer walk with him through the flowering lanes and fields, visiting those warm-hearted neighbors where they were ever made welcome. She was four years younger than her prospective husband, having been born in Kentucky, the State of his own nativity, in January, 1813. When her family removed to New Salem in 1824 she was accordingly in her eleventh year. On the authority of Herndon she was of the noted family of Rutledge of South Carolina, where her father, James Rutledge, was born, and it appears, on the credit of the same sponsorship that she was granddaughter of Edward Rutledge, leader of the four delegates from the Palmetto State to the First American Congress, and signer of the Declaration of Independence. In her veins therefore flowed the blood of Liberty-loving stock whose patriotic ardor had been intensified under the Revolutionary roar of the cannon which made the country Free and Independent. Possessed of a rare mind and disposition in which all the charms of her sex seemed to unite, she was also a person of native, or inherited, refinement, in harmony with the strength and scope of her mental endowments. The qualities of her great forebear seemed to be centered in her intellect and winning personality. There were other children of James Rutledge, younger than she, who was the eldest; several brothers and sisters. Next to her in age was David, a bright and promising young man, in mind and disposition much like his sister. He studied law, was admitted to the bar and gave every evidence of a brilliant career, one that would shed lustre on the Revolutionary name of his ancestor, but he passed away early, dying in 1842 in his twenty-seventh year. His remains lie in the same little grave-yard by the side of his beautiful and gifted sister, who had passed away seven years before, in August, 1835.

When Lincoln first met Miss Rutledge she was nineteen years of age. Her brightness, vivacity and unusual intelligence had made her from early girlhood a general favorite, and among the people of the community there was always a cheery welcome when she tripped into their homes.

Every settlement, especially in small village, or country district, has its social favorite among the juniors of the female sex, usually the brightest and most intelligent, who is held up by the elders of the household and the children as well, as one whose presence radiates joy and sweetness from a charm of personality which is easier to recognize than to define. Of such was she, whose loveliness and amiability made her universally popular, one whose presence, in the community of hardy settlers about New Salem in the crude early days of Illinois, rendered the lives of the people more heartsome and pleasant. Her goings and comings and doings in the community were matters in which everyone, male and female, old and young, felt an affectionate personal interest. As may be supposed, in a region remote from large centres of population, where all were busy rearing homes and providing for a hopeful future, when the people found one of the gentle sex who, more than any other, met with universal acceptance in their regard and affections, she was forthwith idealized, hailed as it were, as a Queen without sceptre, whose gentle sway was spiritual rather than temporal.

Such was the young woman Abraham Lincoln, universal favorite himself, among the hardy people of the New Salem community, was to have led to the marriage altar. Their mutual tastes, capacities of mind, and their dispositions were such that all who knew them, hailed the prospective union as one eminently suitable, with every promise of future happiness.

Her condition, after her return from school, gradually became worse, and, to her family and friends it was evident she was in a sure decline. When the day came that she could no longer walk with him but must lie on a cot in her waning strength, his heart was well-nigh broken and he was thereafter almost constantly at her side. He had become engaged to her in the Spring of 1834. Within less than a year she passed away as he sat by her couch.

The grief of Lincoln has been described by those amongst whom he lived, who were witness to its effects upon him, few believing that his mind would ever regain its former poise. He threw to the winds the cares of business and spent the greater part of the time beside the little mound beneath which the remains of his beloved reposed in the small cemetery near the hill. As he passed to and from the grave he was as silent as the place of sepulture itself, except for his mumbling, half-articulate speech, forsaking all his old haunts and looking the heart-broken young man he was. For almost a year he brooded, and wandered in his mind, spending long hours sitting by the grave and gazing with fixed eyes upon it as one who had lost every interest and aim in life, and only sought to dwell apart from men and think of her to whom his heart-strings had been so bound. Always lean, he grew more thin and gaunt and hollow of eye and cheek. As winter came and the heavy snows spread their blanket of white over the face of

Illinois, the grief of the bereft lover was intensified by the thought impressing itself on his sensitive mind, that she must lie beneath the depths of the frozen mass which shrouded the little grave, saying plaintively to the people with whom he conversed that "She must be cold out there with all the snow over her." His fancy, in this respect, greatly increased his distress, especially as the winter following her death and burial was one of great severity in the West, and the cheerlessness of the new country, before the era of Railroads and the Telegraph, as it lay like a vast white frozen sea as far as eye could reach, was an added burden to his soul's misery. In days when the settlers could not move outdoors except with difficulty,—and then only to feed and water their animals,—he would sit by a window and gaze over the great white drifts in the direction of the grave-yard, speechless in the agony of his grief, except at intervals when he would break the silence to lament that she was there, alone in all the dreadfulness of the savage winter's rigors. The dumb, inarticulate sorrow expressed by weary eyes and sunken cheeks, affected his friends and acquaintances, men and women, old and young alike, not one but whom knew his heart's story, and, in a measure, bore a share of his grief as their own. They were living through tragic days because one of their best and most helpful had fairly lost his reason through grief and his gloom and melancholy affected them all.

At length his friends became anxious through fear his mind would succumb utterly and they sought in many ways to distract his attention and enlist his interest in worldly matters. He was finally induced, through a gentle conspiracy on the part of the kindly people, who knew him and loved him and who felt he would never recover from his grief so long as he dwelt on the spot where he was confronted with daily reminders of his loss, to a pay a visit to valued friends several miles removed from New Salem, Mr. and Mrs. Bolin Green. Their farm was one of the best in the neighborhood and Mrs. Green was known throughout the community as a fine housekeeper and for the excellence of her cooking. Once brought under their hospitable roof the kindly hostess set about to restore the emaciated frame of her guest, who had for months deprived himself of wholesome nourishment and whose thin cadaverous appearance was pitiable to behold. She would prepare the dishes he liked best and sought in many ways to stimulate his appetite, and otherwise uplift him and awaken in him a sense of cheer. The genial presence and conversation of his friend, Bolin, who had long been one of his intimates, also helped revive the fallen spirits of the grief-burdened man, and, coupled with the kindly ministerings of the family, there were frequent visits of young people to the house,—a phase of the conspiracy,—and invitations to appleparings and corn-shucking and neighborhood merry makings in general, to all of which Lincoln must accompany his host and hostess. The methods employed proved efficacious, though at times, in the midst of merriment, he would lapse into deep abstraction of mind and speak of the little cemetery by the hill and say, in a half-stifled groan, "My heart is buried there!"

His long-time law-partner, Herndon, in his description of the means employed to divert him at this crisis in his young manhood, says:

"Mr. Lincoln, in September, went down to Bolin Green's in consequence of the pressure thrown on him and around him, and in the space of a week, or ten days, by Bolin's good humor, generosity and hospitality, his care and kindness, aided by the womanly sympathy, gentleness and tenderness of his wife, Lincoln rose up a man once more. He was visited daily by men, women, boys and girls whose conversation, stories, jokes, witticisms, fun and sport, roused the man, enabling him to throw off sorrow, sadness, pain and anxiety. They walked over the hills with him, danced for him, read for him, laughed for him and amused him in a thousand ways."

Herndon says further in his little book, now out of print and very rare, found only in the hands of collectors:

"Dr. Jason Duncan, of New Salem, about September, 1833, had shown and placed in Mr. Lincoln's hands the poem called in short, now, 'Immortality' or properly, 'Oh Why Should the Spirit of Mortal be Proud?'  *  *  *  Mr. Lincoln went back to New Salem (from Bolin Green's) a changed, a radically changed man. He now once more took up and read and reread the poem and saw new beauties in it. He learned it by heart and repeated it over and over to his friends.  *  *  *  Miss Rutledge died on the 25th of August, 1835, and was buried in Concord Cemetery, six miles northwest of New Salem. Mr. Lincoln has said that his 'heart was buried there,' and in addition, 'I cannot endure the thought that the storm and snow should beat on her grave.' He never addressed another woman 'Yours affectionately,' and generally and characteristically abstained from the use of the word 'love.' That word cannot be found more than half a dozen times, if that often, in all his letters and speeches since that time. He never ended his letters with 'yours affectionately,' but signed his name 'Your friend, A. Lincoln.'  *  *  *  A friend of mine, whose judgment I respect, has said: 'If Mr. Lincoln had married Ann Rutledge, the sweet, tender and loving girl, he would have gravitated, insensibly, into a purely domestic man; locality, home and domesticity were the tendencies of Mr. Lincoln; the love and death of the girl shattered his purposes and tendencies; he threw off this infinite grief and sorrow and leaped wildly into the political arena as a refuge from his despair.' "

The end of his sorrowful brooding came gradually, and he once more began to show interest in practical affairs and in men and things about him. But the seal of sorrow that had stamped its impress on his face remained, the indelible mark of grief over the loss of his first love, throughout his life; not even the admiration and glowing tributes of the millions of his grateful fellow-countrymen who acclaimed him the Saviour of the land in the time of its greatest stress as a free Republic, being sufficient to smooth out the lines of the sad, expressive countenance from which shone the deep-set eyes with the expression of the same heart-touching melancholy with which they had so long contemplated the little mound that marked the spot where lay the remains of Ann Rutledge. And, from the grief-chastened heart sprang those innumerable manifestations of tenderness and sympathy for the sorrows of others, with the unfailing evidence of large Charity in all things, that marked his career as President during his country's most stressful, tragic and harrowing period since the days when it first saw the light through the murk of blood and smoke and fire, as an Independent Nation.

If the work herewith shall serve to illuminate in the mind of the reader, the bright, sun-lit period in the life of the then unknown Lincoln, albeit with its attendant extreme of profound gloom—which transforms his supreme joy into the dark spell of tragedy—and to acquaint him or her in some slight measure with the depths of his nature, its capacity for silent suffering, coupled with the patriotic zeal and high aspirations for usefulness to his fellowmen which stirred in the days of young manhood in the breast of him who lived to become the Great Emancipator, who stands side by side in the pageantry of history with Washington, and who passed, a Martyr to the cause of the preservation of his country and the Freedom of a race of millions, the present work will not have been in vain.

THE AUTHOR.

# ANN RUTLEDGE

## Heart Story of the Early Lincoln

### I

*The grief-stricken lover at the couch of his promised Bride—Her sympathy for him in his distress and her forgetfulness of self.*

Ann Rutledge lay uprais'd on couch of pain:
Frail was her form and thin the shapely hands,
Blue vein'd and white, e'en as two tinted shells,
And faintly transparent, with tips of feather-touch,
In lightness scarce of earth, yet plied with grace unwittingly
As twin'd they languidly, in blank abstractedness,—
As in heart-rest and peace,—strands thick of tangled hair,—
Dark, disorder'd and uncar'd of late,—
Of one of loose-knit frame, on bended knees bow'd low,
Who silent held, close-pillow'd 'gainst his breast,
The fair young head, with brow that soft velour
Of snowy sheen might'st match and sense of beauty charm,
Wherefrom ringlets bright of rippling locks of brown,
O'er shoulders streaming thick, anon didst lightly brush
The lean bronz'd cheeks, wet with slow trickling tears;—
A form in contrast strange wherein was giant strength,
Tho' worn and broken now, as if life's vigor failed;—
And stature mark'd, which, e'en tho' kneeling showed;
And supple,—of ample joint,—as one born on earth to bear
Drear weight of others' loads, with ne'er rasping note of plaint
O'er task impos'd, since inward, fathomless,
Were cheer and heart for all who o'er life's way didst fare,
Which made on shoulders young e'en heavy burden light.

13

The youthful Lincoln he, in morning sun of years
And bounding hopes, tho' e'en long inured
To strenuous toils and world's harsh buffetings,
Withstood with steady head and soul undaunted, e'er,
And faith undimm'd and fond aspirings fair.
   Of nature heartsome, helpful, his,—e'er the friend in need
To sore-tax'd housewives round,—helpmeets of pioneers,—
As to toiling mates;—respected, sought, pois'd high in staid regard,—
Object of special liking, welcome in ev'ry home
Where gladness his coming brought, and sense of vast content,—
As if all worth of Life,—the founts of Destiny,—
In him were met, allaying vague unrest,—
As dawn of sometimes magic-day when care doth vanish quite,
Leaving heart elate to marvel o'er its lift;—
So presence his to them, thro' something innate in him
That touched and pleased, yet baffled,
Leaving stirred deep chords from cause all undefined.
   In worldly wealth, poor as the poorest, he,
Yet rich in favor warm of those 'mongst whom he lived,—
With young and elders all holding place unique,
Owning kinship to none yet claim'd by all as theirs.
And now bows he the couch beside in grief's drear heaviness,
He, of mother-love and tendence early reft,
His childhood life to pass with kindly ones and win
With willing hands and helpful e'er his rugged way,
His mind in accord set, with ready will conjoined,
Youth's problems all to face and fight his battles on
When lo! the marvel hap'd, and sunlit-glow illumed
The heart-recess and mad'st him know a greater, deeper, self,
As she, unthought, didst dawn and all his being fill,
With life thenceforth a thrill,—she Sorceress who ope'd
Clogg'd streams of pent affections deep, releasing thus the flood
That him engulf'd, in whose ambrosial depths
Sunn'd he thro' hours bright in magic change there come
Him to uplift, transmute, refine in wondrous way,
Thro' touch of hidden springs, e'en to the uttermost.
   Thus he, until, like low'ring storm on fairest sky that breaks,
This darkness fell, steeping in gloom his soul,
Unmanning sturdy self that e'er glad strength had known,
Rend'ring blank his life with ne'er a hopeful gleam,

Save living spark here shown and flick'ring day by day,
Where now he bends and her unto him clasps,
Holding tense, e'en as a guerdon dying fingers clutch
To make sure pass to Heaven.  And, on his ears, as a rapt melody,
Her voice did pour in cadence low a full heart's offering;
And wistful were her eyes, of sweet, beseeching tenderness,
As of a wounded deer when, prostrate, it looks upon
Its would-be slayer and moves him till he fain would weep,
As turns he his head away to still the rising flood.
    She, of long heroic line, high daughter of brave Rutledge blood,
Great Edward's grandchild fair, of that illustrious brood,
With Laurens, Marion, Pickens link'd in South Car'linian clime
Who mighty parts didst play in land's upheaval vast
When Tyrant-will defied and Tyrant-strength o'erbore,
Whose names, with others join'd, as struggling Nation's sons,
As orb of Heaven shine in vision infinite,—
As in undying mem'ry;—he, noted forebear bold,
His lofty stand to take as Leader, Spokesman, Counsellor,
Heading chosen four from rous'd dominion sent
To join Assemblage high of sturdy Colonies,
In patriot-city fam'd, by stately Delaware,
Where he, with others great, didst in that Council sit,
And there, in wisdom deep, evolve immortal scroll,
The Declaration high, wide Christendom to thrill
And cheer oppress'd, where'er, the universe throughout;—
He, sterling forebear hers, whose manual sign doth show
In pride of place 'mongst great Car'linian names.
And she, descendant high of noted Rutledge blood,
Offshoot fair of self-same lordly tree,
Her grandsire's spirit hous'd and e'er in acts and words
Didst love of country show, and broad intelligence,
In unison with sense discerning, mark'd, acute,
Of storied stress and trials by which were won the boon.
So priz'd by patriot heart, of glad land's Liberty.
    And to New West came she, as sweet exotic spray,
By careful gard'ner brought,—by fruitful soil allured,—
And there, 'neath sun and air of free salubrious clime,
Didst thrive and bloom to winsome womanhood;
And soon came suitors thick, the choice of country 'round,—
The brains, the wealth, the caste,—their ardent claims to press,

As sang they her praises loud and clamored for her smiles,—
She, goddess there and shrine, to thrill'd and throbbing train,
All by her charms enrapt, and each with heart of hope.
   But she, of mind discerning and of sense discreet,
Unspoiled, their plaints did hear, and yet her heart reserved,
Until succum'd at last in tentative consent,
Which came to naught in end, with her distangled, free,
Until at last, thro' Fate, inscrutable, came he,
The one of all, in mind and heart, where lay
That which she long'd, and, in love of him was peace.
   Alas! that mortal bliss is as the luscious fruit,
Delicious, exquisite, that early perisheth,
As with him it was, of high devoted soul,
For she full soon didst know thro' innate cognizance
With those, beloved of Heaven, from mystic source endowed,
That, pledg'd troth, despite, ne'er for her could be
The wedded joys that loved and lover know
Thro' sun and cloud, but as the child of God.
Hence soon must pass and leave an earthly void
That Time nor change couldst fill, and, to him, bereft,
Bring woe so deep as didst for season threat
The mind's dull lapse—for time e'en shaken much.
   And he, lank and large of bone, with crown of coal black hair,
Unsmoothed, with locks half-screening massive forehead, white,
Thus found his world slipt from him, save one bless'd spot
Where time wast now all centered; for, what was life to him
If she were ta'en?—he, her suitor, late,
For, tho' he long had lov'd, another held the place
And he the boldness lack'd that serv'd his rival well,—
A glitt'ring one, smart in ways and speech,
From East late come, with clothes of stylish cut,
Plausible and bland, free making there with all
Since 'mongst them thrown—they hardy pioneers,
From the four winds, who for their lov'd ones wrought
On Illinoisian wastes, adding unwittingly to country great,
A country greater still, in vasty lands all unbounded spread,
Like a wide sea far Westward reaching, 'yond most distant range
Of human vision, e'en tho' cunning lens didst aid;—
Yea! farther than bright Sol in earth's diurnal rounds
Couldst, thro' man's device for marking flight of time

By hand and dial-plate, hold fix'd his tally-mark,
E'er needing shift of point as space didst supervene,
As neath his glare th' terrestrial planet raced
And show'd, new cleared, the fields and homesteads rude
On fringe of which didst broken one and his heart-treasure dwell.
   Oh, had he spoken in due season there
What years of sorrowing and young life's early blight
Might all been spared! For he, first to win her untried heart
Had faithless prov'd,—impostor held, of borrowed name
Who vanished e'en as came—whither none did know
Nor care, save she, whose pledge he won only thus to break
And so leave poignant wound unhealed until came he, unlooked,
Kindly ministering, worshipper in secret long
And welcome found thro' door of Pity, rekindling in her breast
The heart's dead flame, and there, as earnest wooer sought
Her sacred pledge, the boon that all his being buoyed
With brightest hopes, which, in time he won
With reservation that a year at least should be
Ere they would wed, assent to which he grudgingly did yield.
   Meantime, with her in distant town in care of brother, tall,
In noted school, the time did lag away
And she came home, tho' not the robust girl
To them once known, but delicate and pale
As a blighted flower, when the winds of East
Too rudely blow from ice-bound Scotia's coast;
And Lincoln, into whose life was come this joy of love,
Transforming to an Eden all the wild frontier,
Making rose-tint a world that erst was sere and drab,
Didst feel his being soar, until he saw how wan,
How changed she was, when swift his heart went down
Like leaden plummet that the hardy sounder casts
O'er wave-washed gunwale, and he groan'd within
With prescience sure of his drear loss to be.
   And day by day, e'er looming by her side,
Her steps to aid, was he, as in slow walks they fared
O'er paths, to childhood dear, where ev'ry sapling spoke
Of times now past when she, slim merry pupil, skipt
With lightsome mates o'er wonted beaten way
To low-roof'd school, whose small rectangle housed
Of youth and wit such store,—the young brain-nursery;

Thence homeward trudg'd when golden sun was low
And all were glad in mellow light of sky and field,
To varied chores which little hands well knew
In these plain homes, illumed by love and cheer.
So they, lover-like, the way didst tread of those
Whose lives join'd were to be, and parting know no more,
Save o'er length of years when both were old and gray,—
A pleasing fancy they did cherish, knowing it as such
Yet ne'er each to other owning, until her weakness grew
And she with him could walk the fragrant paths and lanes no more.

# II

*Lincoln voices his woe and forecasts his own death if she shall pass from him. Her rejoinder, dwelling on the shortness of life, and drawing a comparison.*

Then on her couch she lay, of strength her body shorn,
Yet, in spirit same, e'en more entrancing sweet,
And he did e'er attend her, the centre of his world
In her zoned waist there bounded, she his only thought,
For now pretence had vanished and drear reality
Bade him make most of time while yet the slender thread
Didst haply hold. And he in voiceless agony,
As one that stands on crumbling isle and to frenzied bosom clasps
That which to him is life, all that heart holds dear,
While angry waves dash high and ev'ry refluent sweep
Makes waning foothold less, was helpless, with brain in futile rack,
For something yet untried that might, as magic art,
Arrest decline and bring a hopeful change;
Yet conscious e'er how vain such quest must be.
And she, resigned, looked not on life as once,
But gazed beyond, and show'd in her deep eyes
A vision'd peace, and all more winsome seemed
In sight of him, though in that wast shown his doom.
And, he kneeling now, her head upon his breast
And her wan fingers, his thick locks gliding through,
Or stroking lean wet cheeks, in broken accents spoke:
  "Do not, O love of mine, bid me despair!
"Your words I scarce can bear: they cloud my world with gloom!
"If you do go I cannot stay,—I too shall die,
"For what is left to me? My promised bride—my all
"Reft from me! As branching-tree in raging storm is rent
"By lightning-stroke in halves, so this would be to me!
"If you do pass, all desolate am I.
"Despoiled of all and lost, bearing a cureless wound!
"A wanderer o'er the earth, I e'er about would roam
"Aimless, homeless, with no friendly roof nor hearth of cheer,
"And, like the sighing winds my lips would ever moan

19

"For my lost love, until the wearied, wasted frame
"That hous'd such load of grief would sink to earth and die.
"These arms are strong, and in them lives a will
"To toil, and ne'er cease effort glad, to make
"Such joyous life for you,—a dream!—an ecstacy!—
"Fair as the golden beam that in our nest would stray,
"And win yet honors high to make you proud of me;
"Whilst roaming garden bright in rounding scented air        [mignonette,
"And tendence sweet on fragrant plants,—the rose, forget-me-not and
"And others, loved by you—would be your utmost task;
"And we our lives would live with ne'er my zeal relaxt
"In home so dear the world would hold no spot
"With it to match—a Paradise on earth!—
"Till Age's evening came and lengthened shadows fell
"Across the path of years and bade us look beyond
"The Earthly bourne and see the light that holds
"For all who right'ous live, to lead our footsteps hence."
Then she, with lashes wet and eyes full sweet and sad:
    "My friend, husband of my heart,—husband in world to be!
"This life on earth is short!—a little page of print
"Between two covers,—the beginning and the end
"Of a brief sum of thought,—and, the page torn out,
"Goes flutt'ring down the winds, its own design attained,
"Whate'er its fate thenceforth; for it has served its use,
"Transmitting thoughts that live and pass like flash of light
"To other minds and consciousness, which was its mission, sole;
"And when it blows away 'tis as an empty shell
"Here and there to lie, purposeful no more.
"I have liv'd on earth my little fitful day
"And done my lowly part according to my light,
"Helpful, I hope, to others in small and kindly ways,
"With wish for good to all, happy in others' happiness,—
"Ne'er so light and joyous as when some soul thro' me was glad,
"Finding in that my pleasure:—loving and being loved,
"And in sweet confidence and such affections true
"Feeling oft-times exalted, as one who hath foretaste        [pass
"Of bliss of Heaven; and—grieve not my friend!—I soon must surely
"Leaving those most dear, joined to life from infancy.
"They too will grieve, O love of mine! yet they will live and bear
"My passing, and so, dear of my soul, must you,—

"The latest come into my deep heart-house
"And most precious!—you divinely sent to rouse my breast within
"Such flame of joy and sweetness! I do love you, mine!—
"Yes, love the noble, manly strength in you,
"Join'd to such heart of tenderness and sympathy,
"In men so rarely seen; and I do love your thoughtfulness,
"Your high intelligence, your aspirations—all!
"Your goodness, gentleness and devotedness, unselfish, pure!
"So I entreat you bear this parting!  Oh, sweetheart mine, be calm!
"Look on my passing as one enlarged in liberty
"To come and go, and realize our vows shall full meaning know
"When both have pass'd from mortal prison-house
"To larger, purer life that soul unfettered waits;
"For I do believe that, like the page of print,
"Those promptings deep that come to us from source invisible,
"Bespeak a wondrous world beyond, which earthly clamor hides,—
"As a clos'd house, with curtains drawn, so shuts from outward eyes
"The sight of those within whose music, faintly heard,
"Doth tell of gladness there, which may alike our hearts rejoice,
"E'en tho' without, if we of pettiness ourselves divest
"And give to higher things full let, to soar with them in harmony!
"So, those faint-whisper'd counsels, heard within our being deep,—
"Heard and not heard, for they scarce seem dream-echoes of a voice,
"Yet, by sense more deep and subtle mark'd, and, by inner hearing
"To vibrate on consciousness from source unknown, remote,—    [caught,
"Tell of life beyond where holds a fixt and sure design
"To crown our hopes and longings full, if we but hear and heed;—
"Else why shouldst longings be,—why those inmost promptings strong
"That come to us e'en like the noontide bell
"The throbbing air that cleaves to call the toiler from the field
"To sweet repast and respite, with brief absorbing peace,
"Partaker thus of larger, deeper peace to come
"When earthly toils are o'er and soul enlarged doth pass,
"E'en as a ray in some dark place that darts,
"Thro' interstice, howe'er small, from glorious sun o'erhead!
"And so our love shall live when all this earthly dross
"That holds us briefly here is cast and we pass essential, purified."
    Like tone of silv'ry bell the music on his ear
Did seem to linger when her lips had ceased,
And left him straining as if to haply catch

A tremor faintly vibrant still of that which had so thrilled
His being.  At length, in husky voice, as if come from afar,
Or from deep recess dark that him imprisoned held,
He spoke, impressive, 'neath his weight of woe:
  "If you go from me there can never be
"One hour's peace nor happiness on earth for me.
"All I have known that e'er didst give delight
"Will be as fount run dry, to gush from earth no more.
"This heart that late was setting such glad sail
"For Life's sweet voyage, ne'er more shall know a home,
"But dull and aching, a load within the breast,
"Its every throb will strike like dull and senseless stone;—
"A vessel useless, save to keep in pain
"Him who bears, when death alone is peace.
  "Since first I lov'd, what life! what joy was mine!
"Let kings have thrones and men be Croesus-rich!
"Let gilded palace shine, and marble mansion gleam,
"And rank and power flaunt as high as Heaven's dome
"I envied them not one,—nay, felt how poor were they
"Compared with me in wealth of my heart-treasure here!—
"Uplifting me, until from feet and limbs
"Would vanish heaviness, and I then would seem
"On air alone to move, a thing of air in truth,
"Amaz'd o'er lightness felt, translated, as I believed
"Unto a higher plane where soul the body ruled
"And earth and sky were mine, in heart's dominion held.
  "And oft the path I walk'd o'er which your feet had strayed
"That I might in fancy with you be, each plant and leafy shrub
"That lined the way, to me e'er precious, holding meaning tense of you
"Whose dress perchance had brush'd, and left them thrill'd and glad!
"And, each tree 'neath which you pass'd was as a living thing,
"Speechful of you, vocal in praise and rhapsody!
"Ah, sweet the dress of lawn, the girdle, and all the trim attire
"E'er pictured in my heart!  And e'en the little glove
"That I did find reposing down the lane
"On a green bank where we had sate and talked,—
"What dear token 'tis to me!  Memento precious to my heart, of you!
"And certain scented sprays that decked your wealth of hair!
"Oft like a miser, greedy o'er his gold,
"My hands would touch, and then my heart would thril',

"For, in them was you! and, before mine eyes
"Wouldst come your image and I would talk to you
"Thro' tokens such!  I have them treasured up,—
"Odd little things once yours—and ne'er has evening come          [o'er
"That I my treasure-box have not unlock'd and them ta'en and fondled
"And felt your presence there e'en as 'twere you in life.
"Ask me then not to bear such loss as others may!
"If you go from me joy and peace forever pass,
"And the world as desert waste will empty be."

# III

*She seeks to revive his spirits, but he persists in refusing to be comforted, seeing himself a hopeless wanderer doomed to an unknown grave.*

Again was silence, in which, to those two souls,
The earth stood still, and each did peer afar
Thro' inner vision in depths of mystery,
Absorb'd, intense, profound,—a voiceless prison-house    [thoughts
With corridors and court press'd dense with thronging, clam'rous
'Neath the great one dominant that more insistent grew
For leave to speak, and, thro' her, flute-like, melodious,
The spell was broken as she unto his plaint rejoined:
"I am not worth, dear heart, such sacrifice!
" 'Tis bidden us to not set too much store
"On fleeting things, but shape our spirits so
"Our lives shall be at one with God, the Giver of all good.
"He, his arms outholds to bear us o'er the way,
"To aid our falt'ring steps, enfold us unto Him
"And in our woes bring to us solace sweet
"If we but look to Him and believe, without a doubt or fear;
"And if He takes me, Oh my own! it is not meet
"That you should spoil your life and shut your heart from joy.
    "You have your work on earth,—your part,—a set destiny
"In mortal world to fill, and you may not for this yield up
"The hop'd career so cherished.  Rather pluck more strength
"From heart's bereavement, if so my passing hence shall be,
"And there build fortitude, such as may you truly serve
"In lapse of years wherein—who knows!—some mighty need may come
"For one full tried from great soul-depths, one who has suffered much
"And knows heart-throbs of others!  This is your time of trial
"And bear it well, and think of me as one
"Who waits your coming 'yond, when earthly tasks are done,—
"As she who stands at river's edge with eyes strain'd on the pier
"To greet her lov'd one long'd when from the deck he lands,
"His journey o'er and cheer and welcome there."

24

When ceased her voice, with eyes appealing, sweet,
His head he bent and full on upturn'd lips
Pressed fervent kiss and held her long to him
In rapt embrace, the strain of ecstacy
Relaxing at length to say, in heavy, far-toned voice,
With shake of head and look of hopelessness:
   "The river flows in even course until the swirling flood
"O'erswells its banks and spreads o'er country wide,
"Its peace there broke and wonted bounds o'ercome
"Thro' cause not thro' itself, so this my love for you
"That like a stream in even flow hath thro' the being poured—
"How sweet! how joyous!—must it now be overborne          [proof
"And I remain the same?   I cannot myself remake and hold my nature
" 'Gainst such a loss—a loss beyond my strength to bear.
"The years will circle on and I shall never know
"The happiness that should have been, but, like a wastrel heir,
"His patrimony slipt and he an outcast waif,
"With sorrow's burden deep and smart of mem'ries drear;
"Shall plod the weary ways, avoiding haunts of men,
"Lest deep wound bleeding shows and idle talk invites
"When silence alone is bearable—the sentinel that guards
"The trebly-sacred gate, which, broken thro' and seen
"Were desecration—as tho' the form by me so loved
"Were torn from 'neath the tomb and spirited away;—
"And so go ever aimless,—blindly stumbling on
"Until the end, far in some lonely wild,
"Where men shall stare and all in denseness muse
"O'er hapless one, with ne'er a thought such clay
"Once housed a love that might have saved a world."

# IV

*She speaks of the former lover who proved false, and explains the accessory reasons that prompted her to engage herself to him. The glamour of early traditions and images of the golden past.*

His words did move her much and stretching forth her hand
She from her pillow 'neath a dainty kerchief drew
And pressed her streaming eyes until he bent again
And kissed the tears away, with his own lashes wet
And held her to his breast in one long ardent strain,
Her pent bosom shaken and her grief a flood,
For some tense moments' space, when she, at length composed,
With head half-rais'd and retrospective look
In her deep eyes, was silent, in far reflection lost.
Like a grav'd image now, the bronz'd and rugged one,
Save for his shoulders' twitch, which eloquently spoke
Of that astir within, which she, with hands of pity meek
Did seek to soothe as quietly they stroked
His face and hair that noble head encrowned
With poise and mien arresting,—the tense and stalwart frame
In kneeling pose displaying there impressively
A weight of grief beyond relief of words.
 Then she did slightly raise her head and glance
Upon his face, her speaking eyes in search
Of fitting clue to seize and deftly turn
The course of thought, and once again in voice melodious:
 "I have not spoken here of that which you, of all should know,
"Nor sought to justify myself in your dear eyes,—
"For folly of my heart which blinded me to you
"And left me in misery until you did break the spell
"And, thro' your love for me my love didst win and high respect as well.
 "Perchance the feeling I have had 'gainst him,
"Who caused me grief and bitterness, were wholly wrong,
"And I have sought, and made, I hope, my peace with Heaven,
"Filling to full my heart with thoughts of charity
"And taking blame myself for building on false hopes

"The which, I realize, if not o'erturn'd betimes
"Had meant for me a life of wretchedness.
   "He came upon me here in these far Western wastes,—
"From polished cities far and land of culture fair,—
"To this dim world where all is crude and new,—
"And made for me an East, where grand traditions dwell
"And people glorified,—the birth-place of our race
"And, of him revered, the mighty prop and stay
"Of Patriot-hopes in dreariest, darkest hour,—
"The wise, illustrious, great, as Country's Father known,
"Long since at rest by lov'd Potomac's shore,
"'Midst scenes endeared, beneath the solemn tomb,—
"The shrine of shrines where all make pilgrimage
"To seal their vows of faith in what his life expressed.
   "And not on him alone, high patriot and peer
"Of Earth's transcendant ones, my thoughts would oft-times turn:
"Those other shining souls who in great hour stood
"And lives and weal all pledged on that immortal scroll
"That 'roused the World's amaze and thrill'd remotest lands
"By just defiance high of Royal Tyrant's will
"And Tyrant's right to stamp the heel beneath
"The God-Created Free, a gage of war to death,
"Cheering Earth's opprest and rearing Hope aloft,—
"How they resplendent shine and deepest rev'rence claim!
   "What wonder, then, if oft my mind did long,
"And all my being thrill with tense o'erwrought desire,
"To breathe the air of that enchanted realm,—
"To tread the soil by great ones hallowed so!
"He—he came to me and with his coming brought
"All I had imaged of the distant coast
"That Jamestown's settlers knew, or yet more rugged shore
"Where Plymouth's waves dash high, and thro' whose mists I saw,
"As vision strange that comes to one in dreams,
"All those dim pageantries,—the Puritan austere,
"Chin tilted sharp and eyes averted e'er
"O'er sinful ways and all unhallow'dness:
"Environment all gray, which pure devotedness
"Did make as ermine rich;—his goings, comings, all
"Weird scenes and ways that tomes of hist'ry fill
"Of land's beginnings,—to me most wonderful!—

"Those early trials where savage fierce and wintry blast assailed
"And lives tragic made of gently-nurtured ones
"Who heaving seas had brav'd with faith assured in God,
"Enduring hardships unheard for hardships greater still,
"All, all for Liberty, and right to live and worship free
"From Tyrant-rod and Tyrant minions, fell;—
"Those dark-garbed men and saintly women, pure,
"Erect and spare of frame, as they who keep strict fast
"On Holy Day; and they of later growth of that same lineage, they,
"The learned, cultured, great,—poets, philosophers,          [rang
"Whose thoughts do light New World, and they whose Patriot-voices
"Thro' early hall and forum,—Giants of Debate,
"And shining ones in Statesmanship, whose tones for Freedom thrill
"Yet in our ears and make glad our hearts that we
"Do own a Past so great and glorious!
    "And I had lived and reveled in the thought of these,
"E'er loving my School Readers, so much that made of them,—
"In fancy heard the bell in thrilling tones proclaim,—
"To Earth's remotest bounds, thro' air vibrating shrill,—
"Sharp sev'rance of the chain, by fell Oppression forged
"To bind full-statured men and break them to its will.
"And I had read, re-read and conn'd the lessons o'er
"In that fam'd city taught,—our Freedom's Fountain-head,—
"Home of the self-same Bell, the Flag and Declaration great:—
"Scene of those early acts that bring such glow of pride
"To ev'ry Patriot-cheek,—and had thought to see them all
"As a home-coming bride, thinking less of him
"Than of the glamour of his native coast.
    "Thus I had weaved about me figures of the past,
"And fantasies, mayhap, that round the real do cling,—
"Those unsmiling churchly ones, flint-locks on shoulders poised,
"As forth thro' winter-gloom trudged they, with faces white and set.
"Wives and little ones close-grouped, with eye and ear alert,
"Lest lurking foe, with knife and tomahawk should spring
"And take their cruel toll, as oft in truth they did.
    "What trials, what deep heart-wrenchings theirs, who may fitly tell!
"What suff'rings tense on wintry coast when Arctic blasts did drive
"From frigid zone o'er wat'ry wastes and frozen isles afloat,
"Sending chill on chill thro' shiv'ring frames already numb,
"Yet e'er withstood with calm, as early Martyrs e'en

"At stake or pill'ry vile, by flame and lashings tried,
"Their spirits there, as here, by more than mortal will upstayed!
　"And I have seen, in fancy, too, the early Jamestown ones
"In misty past on their dim coast by same grim perils faced　　[Red,
"As swarmed both stream and forest dark with those wild warriors,
"Stoics of New-World kind, to Mercy stranger, quite,　　　　[told.
"On blood and pillage bent, as dripping scalps and blazing homes oft
　"And, the blood mirage past, I have lived thro' later days and scenes
"When they had pressed the savage back and all the land the Virgin
"For aye commemorates, had from its night emerged　　　[Queen
"To dazzling day, e'en as a gem, all cleansed and polished bright
"That charms the eye and wins full meed of praise.　　.
"Ah! had she, from whom that clime derives its name so sweet,—
"Its consonanted sounds like tinkling silver on the ear,—
"Had life prolonged and in mind's vigor seen
"The shining greatness of the sons it bore
"How proud she must have been, and, with what gladness then
"She might have passed, leaving such memorial of her reign!
　"How thrill'd was I o'er thought of joyousness in store
"To live and move and breathe in that illustrious realm
"Which knew the early Great, far from these unstoried plains
"Where books were few and chance of learning slight!
"And how I yearned and wished that those fond dreams were true
"And not mere fancy-films! And then—he—he—came as though
"My prayer was heard and granted, and when he asked my hand
"My heart ne'er knew such joy, with my whole being steeped
"With love and longing for those things I soon was now to know
"In that glad life, to my fond vision shown,
"Where those bright beings dwelt whose raiment I might touch,
"Whose voices I might hear, and whose sweet radiant eyes
"Might gaze perchance in friendliness upon me. Thus I had dreamed.
　"He profess'd and promis'd much and I did trust him full
"Till he departed hence, and then, as a dark-vision'd spell
"That holds one horrified, there came upon me here
"Vague rumors and surmise, later verified by proof,
"That he was not what he had claimed, but had feigned a part
"Which made his life a lie, not e'en the name he gave
"Being his in truth, and, with these, my airy castle fell
"And left me of cherished hope bereft, my longings forfeit quite.
　"They sent me hence, as well you know, thinking I would forget

"Amidst new scenes and peoples, but my wound was deep
"And, my friend, 'tis mortal!  Your dear love for me
"Doth come too late to save, although my humbled heart
"Is yours indeed, and in this blessed hour,
"I feel a joy too much, I fear, for the tenuous thread
"That holds me here.  Though I shall never know
"Those bright beings longed, and scenes my fancy framed
"I have what now surpasses all in this, your love for me,
"And in my love for you, so my cup of happiness is full."

# V

*In her effort to divert him from the cause of his distress she predicts his future, giving reasons for her belief in a great destiny in store for him—Lincoln impressed by her words makes reply, touching on the tragedy that entered the Lincoln house and carried off his grandfather—expresses the belief that he is heir to woe, yet pays a beautiful tribute to his step-mother.*

Her head lay restful and again he stooped
With gently ope'ing arms as if a child to clasp
And kissed her cheek, enfolding her to him,
His answer there to her all-moving speech
And ne'er releasing until she gently drew
Herself more free, and, weaving unthinkingly his fretful locks,
With her slim fingers, pointed prettily,
In playful twists with love-light in her glance
Saw presently in deep-set eyes the unshed tears
That sorrow spoke more forcefully than words.
　　"Grieve not, dear friend," she said, "for I shall pass and come,
"E'en as the morning mist that lifts and shows a brighter day,
"To raise you up in heart when most you stand in need
"Of cheer and solace; for, I feel assured
"That you are born to rise to some great eminence
"And mayhap fill the land with glory of your name;
"For, I have noted that,—by you all unperceived,—
"As natural quite, in modesty and soul-largeness—which makes me
"How all depend on you, look up to you as guide,　　[marvel much,—
"Seeking counsel oft with faith implicit shown,
"E'en as a family group that in best brother trusts—
"In rectitude of mind, unselfishness of heart,—
"E'er of you regardful, as if within you lay
"Something beyond their ken—a vast intelligence
"And with it a kindliness that wins on ev'ry hand,
"Binding men to you, rousing their pride in you,
"Seeing in you more than you, in diffidence,
"See in yourself,—the Nation here in miniature—
"And you the Leader—by all save you so recognized;
"An intellect that far outstrips all local bound'ry lines

31

"And seems the reflex of a people's mind
"Which, in amplitude does service here for all
"And in reserve leaves rich unmeasured store,
"Causing all to believe, e'en as in gospel creed,          [bined,—
"That none there is like you, in wit and willingness to serve, com-
"Conviction sprung from what your own untiring service proves.
    "And I do realize that in a larger sphere,
"Which you in time shall fill, same traits of mind and heart
"Shall others move as here, and make their impress deep
"On scroll of time.  Who knows!—in years to come
"You too, before all eyes may tow'ring stand
"In country's pageantry,—your face and form imag'd e'en as his
"Whom we revere, and monuments and statues, grand,
"Shine in your honor o'er the land, as those
"That loom for him, who on Mount Vernon's shore
"Sleeps his last sleep whilst live his lofty words and deeds
"As lives the spirit that e'er ruled his life."
    Lincoln then, with eyes new-lit, despite his tide of woe,
Roused by her words did find some cheer of heart,
And, rising erect, with animation drew
His wonted chair, lately thrust aside,
Close by her couch, and thereon sitting, leaned
In forward pose, and stretching forth his hand
There let it rest upon the wealth of hair
That crown'd her head, and found a voice to speak
In other strain, and making truce with gloom, replied:
    "I am not vain enough, dear love, though you might make me so,
"To think of self in line with greatness, but would humbly seek
"My part to do in life and true expression give
"To what is best within me, howe'er small it be,
"That I may reckon up, when Conscience calls to book,
"And show a balance clear in acts of usefulness
'To fellowmen;—no more nor less than this
"Else life be not worth living.  True to oneself and so to others true!
"That rule seems best as guide and I e'er seek to make it mine.
    "Your words have deeply stirred, and I can understand
"Those full heart-yearnings o'er the cherish'd themes
"Dwelt on by you, for I myself have dreamed
"Of Grand and Great and felt the glamour strange
"That clings to them thro' Time's rich mellowings,

"And, when thoughts so turn, there e'er before my eyes
"A figure tow'ring stands ne'er approached by man
"In stature of such greatness, the sense of whose high words,
"Not less than lofty deeds, go ringing down the years
"And so will ring, I think, forevermore.
    "And I have view'd, with eye of mind, that lone impressive tomb
"On old Potomac's shore, his storied natal stream,
"Where grand traditions are, and thought how like it was,
"In simple aspect there, to ways of him in life:
"Elsewhere his monuments, all o'er the country wide,
"Loom high,—in marble, granite and e'er enduring bronze,—
"No site too costly, no price too high for these memorial piles;
"Yet, there at home no chiseled stone nor high-wrought metal marks
"The place he lies, but that plain railing round
"The pebbled earth 'neath which doth rest his clay,
"Speaks more than all in voice of eloquence
"Of his great life, and points the moral so.
    "Fit place of rest!  The ceaseless waves there breaking on the shore
"Their peans sing o'er grave where he, the mighty, sleeps!
"Perpetual music from undying choir,
" 'Neath green magnolia leaf and varied fragrant boughs,
"In quietude intense, from haunts of men remote,
"In that simplicity which Greatness e'er befits,
"Whilst, serene above, the classic mansion shines,
"Abode of calm and peace that blest his closing years,
"Home of great Memories!  Inspiration's fount!—
"Distinctive seat, all in chaste whiteness framed,—
"In style and grace without compare on earth.
    "And I too, in mind have often dwelt upon
"Those long-past scenes down the dim stretch of years
"Where flit the Puritan and others quaint in ways,—
"The Broad-brim meek, of speech and garb distinct,
"In dawn of things that seem as bedded seed
" 'Neath soil to lie and in due season sprout,
"By world unnoted, e'en as the wayside shrub
"That shoots and slowly spreads and fills erst barren waste;—
"So our forebears there who 'neath Time's stratas show,—
"Those solemn forms in drab-like seriousness,
"Stalking vague afar, as figures faint in mist,
"Seeming as phantoms of the wind and air,

"Haunting a phantom coast that e'er doth hear the moan
"Of a weird phantom sea, that all desolate doth lie
"Beyond a gray world's rim,—dream-like, mystical,
"E'en as world and sea that were, and now but legend, mere,
"With old Atlantis' wastes to merge,—or, in Silurian dawn
"To grope and have their day,—those ghostly ones that move
"Thro' eld of New-World strand, and pass and come in groups
"Noiseless and dim, haunts of our vision strange,—
"In lives remote, beyond all touch of us,
"As those marooned on some far distant Isle
"Where waves e'er lash and brightness ne'er appears,
"But gray of sea and waste instead do e'er the prospect fill.
    "So they,—those past!—environment to fit
"Their tenuousness;—wraith-like, intangible,—
"The shell-strewn shore and dim-lit horizon
"Prospect e'er ruling, with flitting figures vague
"Which Moderns, we, from peaks of vast Preoccupation view,
"As dusky,—faint,—groping in Night of things
"E'er for more light,—they, these early ones
"Who oft thro' inner vision show, silent, yet eloquent in mien and look;
"Who come and go, as in bewilderment;—
"O'er waste of sea oft gazing with eyes intent and fixt
"That more than words heart-longings tell, yet steps retracing e'er
"To inland wilds with burden'd dreary consciousness
"That ne'er for them shall faring be beyond
"But heaving main the sight shall bar of native shore
"Where bones of forebears lie, Machpelah cave to them,
"Tho' not as Canaan's son their dust to there repose,
"But reft of land of old new future grim didst loom
"In wild and alien world where they must stifle sobs
"And bend to needful tasks reclaiming wilderness
"Into place fit,—abode of light and air
"And genial warmth, responsive soil to cheer.
    "They won new World and, as the forest passed
"With gnarled and time-worn trunks, passed they, procession-like.
"Stern work their lot, they first to ope the ways
"Thro' young land's gloom and bring a brighter glow
"To soul and mind, and then, departing leave
"Hallowed mem'ries and a goodly fame,
"With base to build and make the structure great.

"How they did toil in those unlighted days
"What ills they knew!—by us of later time
"Scarce realized or dreamed;—from us, how far removed
"In light of modern days and subtleties!—beings so unlike as not to be
"Of self-same species, seeming, but more as spirits breathed
"To life and motion on that misty coast,
"Outlined so vague in mem'ry, as if they ne'er had been,—
"So changed the world since then in which all things have shared;—
"For, they would know us not if they should come to life
"And tread the paths of old where first their steps did stray.
"What 'wild'ring looks then theirs! what speechful questioning
"By eyes and faces, tense, since tongue its part would fail!
"What wonderment supreme! what gaze of eloquence!—
"As if 'twere not the earth they left, but some new planet found
"And peopled by others strange, of ways beyond their ken!
"For, they cast off the mortal shell true to king and throne        [bued
"With ne'er thought that such would change,—with rev'rence so im-
"For Right Divine of Royalty that deep had been the wrench
"Their inmost hearts must know had future then been bared,
"And broken sceptre shown, with offspring dwelling free,
"Enacting laws their own, nor longer awed by regal pomp and power.
    "What shock to them, hadst it so been!—they in doctrine taught
"That each sev'ral cheek must be in mildness turned
"To feel alternate slap by hand of Malice dealt,
"Thus, e'er granting leave to godless kingly crew,
"By usage brutaliz'd, to beat and bruise and break        [press.
"And so encourage those that harsh and cruel are the meek to still op-
    "With what amazement then, couldst they come back and view
"Where home and tenure were,—at base at king's behest,—
"And, there flouted find, and kick'd and bandied high and low
"The name of Royalty and those prerogatives
"Which lorded high and sway'd the land they left
"And kept the mild cheek-turners vieing each with other literally
"In meek observance of that which swells the Tyrant's pride and spleen.
    "As patients then, who from dark room emerge
"With shaded eyes that light may be less harshly felt,        [awaked
"They must needs be led—didst they return—till sense wast new
"And they madst to know the change—they whom we view thro' mist,
"Seemingly unreal, as tree by lengthen'd shadow limned;—
"Who, in vision stir on shoals of Time, so quaint from us in ways

"That we, the far-descended, scarce do seem the same
"In blood and fibre;—they, submissive old, who more as spirits shine.
    "But they were real, those ancient ones, and not the ghosts they seem
"Look'd at thro' centuries gray!—'tis only we who change
"And show a world so alter'd, tho' holding fast to things,
"The ideals high of life those lofty souls conceived,
"Albeit building on base for those who wouldst in time reverse
"That zeal which they, the builders, held for king and crown
'And so pass'd hence, leaving to us the mighty heritage.
    "Their dangers, too, I know, for, did not my grandsire fall,
"Long after they,—e'en lapse of Century's pace twice run,—
"Had toiled and fought the Red Man there and known
"Alternate parts of victor and vanquished—dreary rounds of strife
"Prolong'd and shifted inland, as pale ones stronger grew,
"And e'er unresting pressed toward wider Westward goal,
"My father's sire amongst them, to find his end at last
"In lone Kentucky field, where, creeping up by stealth
"From out the forest dense, as he,—the toiler,—bent,
"O'er harsh-bak'd earth and plied the dull-edg'd hoe,
"Unwarned the foe was on him, and with fearful yell
"And tomahawk, high-pois'd, did strike and lay him low;
"Nor sated e'en with that, but swift with brandished knife
"Did lift the scalp and bear it warm away
"As trophy of the deed, all in red murder done.
    "Thus tragedy must stalk into the Lincoln house,
"And tragedy, I fear, pursue the Lincoln name,
"Till then unscathed, thro' all the run of years
"From early day in Pennsylvanian wilds,
"And e'en before in land of Puritan,
"Of strenuous misty times where all flits shadowy,
"And here am I, the wind-toss'd weathered limb
"Of that scarr'd tree, the lineal heritor
"Of weight of woe from woeful thing derived,
"Whose turn may come in unthought way and hour
"And I fall prone in some calamity:
"For I do feel, of late, that all the world is dark,
"And hardly grope my way without an inward cry
"O'er intense wretchedness,—surprised when others laugh,
"A thing full strange to hear in mood so far from mine,
"And wond'ring what it is that makes men's spirits light,

"And seeing naught but hopelessness, pond'ring why it is
"That I was ever born; yet glimpsing ray of cheer
"O'er thought of her, my mother's place who took,
"And brought us toddling-ones with joy about her knees,
"Op'ing to us her heart and schooling us as well,
"And leaving dark our lives when she did pass away,—
"We of joy bereft, yet with wealth of mem'ries dear,
"And longing that the world, where'er lived people true,
"Might know her excellence,—the Mother that she was."

# VI

*She, still wishing to rouse him from his gloom, enters on a speculation on the slow progress the country has made in settlement and incidentally lauds the bravery of the Indians. He points to the Napoleonic wars and turmoils in Europe as causes that have retarded progress in the New World.*

Then she, whose heart had lightened o'er what him had seem'd to lift
From utter depths, did parry now the thrust
By him self-aim'd, in hope to ward away
Recurring pain and hold his mind upon
The themes he loved in normal state and hour.
  "How strange," she said, "that time so long has lapsed
"Since Jamestown's day, e'en two full Centuries past—
"And more—and finds us here with self-same problems still,—
"If not we, at least those daring ones beyond,—
"The unbroke wilds and that red forest foe,
"Who naught save inches yields and leaves a dreary stain
"The land to dye all its wide area o'er,
"Where hands may later till, and still rich cities rear,—
"Each or both,—with ne'er a thought the while
"How dearly bought the soil by those that silent lie
"With dust commingling fine, the spoil of Cent'ries past;
"And how same process still in manner like ensues,
"From storied early coast to far dim border here:—
" 'Twixt man wild and man illum'd a struggle ceaselessly,—
"One-sided e'er thro' o'erweight of might and train'd intelligence,—
"Advantage unfair, tho' oft, as at Thermopylae,
"A heavy toll the loser taking,—a new Leonidas
"At ev'ry pass and turn,—the flame unquenchable
"That drives the warrior forth to die unheralded
"For cause albeit high and sacred to souls of them
"As e'er to Spartan band who better fortune owned
"In votaries of song heroic deeds to hail
"And so upraise to view thro' Time where eyes of all might see.
  "But he, untutor'd one, who fights for life and home
"And ne'er fears to die in cause by all revered,
"No eulogist doth have, no bard his praise to sing

38

"But all unnoted falls, for mourn of stolid mate,
"In grief not less acute that her set lips are dumb,
"As those of his young braves, their father's eyes no more
"On childish orbs to flash and note with warrior's pride
"The promise in them held,—his deed to pass, as he
"To dark oblivion drear, or, if to light revealed,
"And view of foeman pale, to there be gibed and scorned
"As if no right had he, e'en more than beast of prey
"To strive his home to save and weal of those most dear;—
"A wrong that e'er persists thro' run of hoary years,
"Begun with New-World's breath and held unbroken since,
"With certain doom for him, receding slowly e'er;—
"A fate that cows him not who knows no qualm of fear,
"And hence, in its appeal to what we cherish most
"Shouldst rouse our chivalry, if chivalry there be,
"And, with honors meet, a just amendment bring
"For wrongs to race so brave, in peace and amity
"With former foes to dwell 'neath solemn majesty
"Of Law's protection full, and by example, lift
"To higher plane their lot until of savagery
"No vestige land should know, but all in brotherhood
"The pale and red should be, nor strife betwixt them more."
  Beam'd face and eyes of her with animation there
As pause she made,—such heighten'd loveliness
That he who words hadst drunk didst gaze on her enrapt
For moment tense, then bending low, her cheek didst pat and kiss
In soothing fond caress, and sitting erect at length
Took up the thought where left by her and said:
  "Slow progress we have made, 'tis true, but the world was drained
"By Europe's wars and writhings,—those red years in France
"To which our Lafayette returned, their Revolution fanned
"By breath of those who aided here, tho' that leader held
"True to his king; and then Napoleon came
"And built up on the ashes of the ruined State,
"Only to make more welter still, of wider range
"Yet for all a greater France—vastly enlarg'd, improved,—
"Whilst the world meantime, so rack'd, harassed,
"Stood, as seem'd, stock still, and our new clock as well
"As old-land dial-hands, was stationary too—
"One reacting with like effect on other,—whilst our genius seemed

"For time in full eclipse, our hands too busy then,—
"As child that wondrous plaything has,—in our new toy absorbed,
" 'Yond Coastal fringe to stir; and, for reason other, too,
"That, as forbidden wall,—tho' penetrable hence and yon,
"By those, our daring ones, who utmost risk assumed,—
"Loom'd Appalachian range that countless perils held
"In wild ferocious tribes; and, valiant one was he
"Who, like our Washington, wouldst forth adventure 'yond,
"Save strong with escort arm'd;—he lone exemplar high
"Of spirit brave that all with this dispensed,
"And, with twice-twain helpers there the many dangers faced,
"Crossing fearful zone to land more fearful still,
"Enduring hardships the while 'yond e'er what settler knew,
"In resolution great high mission thus to fill;—
"Resolve 'gainst ev'ry menace proof, as all privations, too,—
"A dauntless soul by Heaven raised, if e'er was man on earth,
"A rigid test to pass all more to shape him wise
"So might he forth emerge in high appointed hour,
"The one of all 'mongst men to compass and effect
"Design of Him from time when stars of morning sang,
"To found a Nation great with mighty charge entrust,
"The shining lead to take with Righteousness its creed
"In practice as in name,—the Brotherhood of man
"Essence of its belief, enduring corner-stone.
    "So he in early day, when early peril loomed
"The frowning range beyond o'er shad'wy journey fares,
"The whisper of the wood, the songs of insect tribe,
"And chirp and trill of birds and distant call of beast,
"Vast silence oft to break and mark drear loneliness
"Of pathless forest-wilds,—the gloom of wilderness,
"Thro' which press'd onward he with e'er unwav'ring aim,
"On set grim purpose bent, high Duty's part to fill
"At dim and dangerous goal, Ohio's waters then—
"Where Allegheny's flood doth south-born sister greet,—
"Monongahela fair,—from mountain fastness come
"Of staid Virginian realm o'er Northward course adown—
"With warlike tribes all dense, a mighty barrier there,
"E'en if pass'd blue-crested range and lowland thence attained
"Free from mishap o'er land of Risk, to greater peril find,
"Since there and onward thence e'en all unchartered lay

"New-World's unmeasured wastes 'yond western horizon
"Vast, o'er bounds of belief in space as in resourcefulness;—
"Not to be sum'd by scope of world the Romans knew
"Nor yet by that which daring son of Philip won,—
"Not e'en by high word Empire in full meaning gauged,
"But by term alone more grand in its significance,—
"A Hemisphere, no less,—which, for cause all adequate,
"To ope and clear a tenth,—much less exploit the whole,—
"Two cent'ries full of time has ta'en and more.
    "So hardly strange it is the lapse such world has claimed
"For spread of pale man's race from place he first appeared,—
"All Christendom itself in throes of Change the while,
"Its people in main upstirr'd by great example here,
"New star in firmament that planets old outshone,
"The torch our forebears lit o'er all Earth to flare
"As rays of Northern lights o'er Polar realm outspread."
    Then she, as paus'd his speech, her head did nod, bright crowned
With wealth of shining hair, and smile and beam on him
And, with mingled wit and seriousness rejoined:
    "I should have culled my words a moment since, perhaps
"To him in deference here who toils of war have known,
"Employ'd 'gainst Chief Black Hawk and hardy tribesmen fierce;
"Yet naught detracts my speech from worth and aim of him,
"The Captain of the band, and meed of those he led
"If I such thoughts express.  Black Hawk and his we know
"To take our lives and burn our homes had of scruple naught,
"So 'twas meet and just our brave should 'gainst him move,
"And, with marshaled might, since other means did fail,
"Him and his tribe o'ercome, howe'er may balance stand.
"Hard task it is the Savage heart to change
"And great the score which he against us holds.
"In days to come, perhaps, the just amend may be
"And wrongs of Cent'ries righted; yet, what field, meantime, is here,
"In theme on which you speak, for mind's inventiveness!
"What boundless great domain for Fancy's playground shown!
"Our shores, two far-spaced oceans wash, vast Continent between,
"One East, whose coast from end to end we know,
"Thanks to Old World's daring ones,—restless Europe's wights
"Whose land lies not remote, wherefrom hies Commerce brisk
"And seeks all places out, e'en almost ere for us began

"Those trials, traditions, tests, by pens all threadbare writ,—    [more,
"Atlantic's fringe reveal'd, no part o'erlooked, no ground for wonder
"Since searchers by thousands summ'd, have Truth from maze of do-
"And dinn'd in ears of all,—the edge from Fiction ta'en,—    [ings digged,
"If Fiction Puritan allow'd,—prospect adverse in truth,
"Since Fancy no chance did have as on the strand he stalked,
"Its new-come master there, who e'er at presence frowned;
"Resentful his spirit stern 'gainst what didst mask the Truth
"And ready e'er to seize the goddess' winsome form
"And hale to Ducking stool and there her name disgrace;
"And lucky she with this, since slight the scruple there
"To charge of witchcraft lay and passion wild inflame,—
"As, there on hill of Salem drear—and faggots high to pile
"Round her, the witch condemned, on idle childish tale
"That wouldst the schoolboy scout in this enlightened day—
"That she,—alack!—was seen high thro' the air to ride,
"A broomstick her aerial car, sent here and there at will,—
"Logic ignoring quite that if she such power had
"What wouldst her then prevent to use her sorcery
"And skim from Court and Judge high in ethereal blue
"With laughter and with gibe, o'er lowly impotence
"To circumscribe the witch, and occult doings curb.
  "Oh, dreary 'tis to view what things mistaken zeal
"May steep the souls of men, intolerant themselves,
"Yet by Intol'rance wrong'd, and driven wide seas o'er
"By Persecution's lash, to build their homes anew
"And there rear altars high whereat to stern effect
"Observance of same ills from which so suffered they
"In land they left behind,—an atavistic lapse
"By cell of brain enforc'd, in which mayhap there lacks,
"Thro' suff'rings in past, that which reaction checks
"But drives the spirit dark to rise and re-enact
"What erst nigh crush'd its life, and then a balance strike
"That Past shall all off-set, and thus vindicate the law
"That tooth for tooth enjoins,—not law of Charity
"But law of vengeance dark that clouds beneficence
"And soul depresses low, howe'er may Purists rage!
  "Two oceans thus, one of storied coast that earliest teachings tell,
"And one o'er sunward way that like a dreamland lies
" 'Neath glorious evening glow, e'er by rapt senses seen

"In Fancy's imagery,—the land of rhapsody
"Where summer dwells for aye and rarest fruits abound,
"And tree and plant and flower show in gorgeousness;
"With birds of plumage rich and wond'rous melody—
"As if of hues of golden sky partaking,—tone and color all,—
"A Paradise to make, whereof its picture-sky
"As seen at eventide our gladden'd hearts to thrill,
"Is only faint reflex;—so seeming from afar;—
"A clime where lightsome goddess reigns and weaves her fabrics fair
"Of which, to us faint shimmer comes, e'en as a mirage glad,
"Our beings to enthrall in mimed reality;—
"Realm whereof may all alike full wise and knowing be
"Since as to what it holds one much as other knows,
"All bound 'neath Fancy's spell,—in her sweet meshes wrapt
"And quaffing 'vidiously from her light golden cup,
"With ready will embellished tales to believe,
"E'en though of endless wealth she dazzling picture draws,
"With gold in rocks and sands and river-courses deep,
"E'en as Golconda rich,—such wax are we her artful hands within
"On this strange theme of vast and shiny land
"Where golden mist enshrouds on coast of summer sea.
  "Such land all mystic then, the home of legend-lore,—
"E'en as Asian wastes,—from us here placed,—remote,
"Whence may store of wonders lie for graphic pen to tell
"Strange as Arabian Nights, which countless minds allure,
"Half fabulous, half real,—romance and poesy
"From beauteous realm there plucked with all its pageantry
"Of blended tints and hues and sacred mysteries,
"To pique our wonder more and set our mouths' agape
"At each fair harbinger that from charm'd clime appears,
"Or claims from there to be;—for, how may we decide,
"Calm Truth and Fiction, 'twixt, since Fancy's freaks we know,—
"She, who e'er from us, in doubt, full benefit receives,—
"At least our impulse so; but she may not complain
"If pause we all anon and face what real before us lies;—
"The inaccessible, the unattainable, as seems
"To sense of all,—in sense who are,—that Fancy's words confront;—
"The lands impenetrable 'twixt us and sunset coast that are,—
"Vast Rocky Range that looms cloud-kissing high—
"The hills, the hollows all, and wilderness besides

"That lands of earth's upheavals know,—where beast and man infest—
"One wild as other is, with no brave Washington
"The dangers there to front, the great fatigues endure,
"As he, through Appalachian wilds the zone of danger pierced
"And Allegheny's stream, where South-born sister meets,
"Didst there attain in rugged, ruddy youth
"And, through all survive, in lapse of years to bless
"His kind, and pass, tho' not in truth to die,
"Since, lives he in ev'ry heart, a force potential still.
    "So let bright Fancy play in field so fine and large;
"O'er mountain-peaks there roam, kissed by her magic sun;
"And let her feast on fruits, the golden apples rare
"And deck her hair with blooms of fragrance exquisite,
"And skim o'er jewelled waves where wide Pacific sleeps!—
"All, all are hers,—her tales we'll not gainsay,
"For, who knows to speak!  So let us be content
"And thro' her jewelled lens view what may or may not be
"Since time may never come when we,—on hither side who dwell,
"Of Rocky Range so vast and high,—the magic land may know;—
"Advantage Fancy has in that her arts may do
"What man may never hope,—e'en scale the mountains high—
"The yawning chasms span,—the raging rivers leap,
"The tow'ring hills pierce thro',—whate'er her will may list—
"Whilst daz'd explorer stands, his pack on shoulders poised,
"Which e'er more heavy grows as dawns the truth on him
"That way seems ever barr'd and naught but Fancy's wing
"May such stern barriers pass to reach the glorious zone;
"But he who wouldst attain must sail o'er treach'rous wastes
"Off Patagonian rocks where e'er opposing winds
"From antipodean lairs in mighty combat meet
"And toss men's playthings high with rending crash of sail,
"The fearsome snap of mast, the hollow vessel's groan,
"And shrieks and prayers of men as in the deep they go,
"Raging waves o'er all to close as fearful screams the dirge
"Of storm and sea above, and calls for victims more.
    "Thus she her ally has, capricious, winsome Sprite,
"That keeps the realm her own, to there disport and play,—
"The nymph that culls such tales and makes the world her own,
"With tears and laughter now, and voiceless awe anon,—
"Whate'er she wills to be,—the mistress of our minds,

"Who oft her role performs despite our sober sense
"That 'gainst her wiles wouldst warn,—persuasive sprightly one,
"Whose voice we e'er do love, whose freaks we e'er forgive
"Since she so lightsome is and winsome e'er as well.
"And, tho' she Fact distorts to most ridic'lous length
"And tells, with smile so coy, that men thro' air may fly
"High o'er the loftiest peaks, dim in the upper blue,—
"O'er rivers, mountains, seas,—and make their journeys safe,—
"Distance and Time both extirpating quite,
"Far lands on earthy-plane no more to them remote,
"And words of mouth may o'er wide realm be sent,
"And e'en 'yond seas for ears afar to hear,
"And there inform, direct, instruct, enlighten full,
"And like in turn receive,—all wizardries of air—
"Where Man, like birds, may soar, than birds e'en higher fly,
"And arts of sound display and turn to human use!—
Whate'er her tales let Charity prevail
"And know that o'er her mask is oft similitude
"Of that which lives in fact, as time in past hath proved,
"Whence born the saw of ancient origin
"That Truth itself more strange than Fiction is!—
"A plume in Fancy's cap howe'er her word we doubt;—
"So, mayhap her stores of gold, mimed by the sunset glow,
"In her enchanted land, may there be strewn in truth,
"And, likewise too, men thro' the air may fly
"An idea persistent e'er since old Daedalious' day
"Despite mishap to him as found in Fable-lore
"With Fancy's imprint plain, the Authoress supreme
"Whose laurels may ne'er be won, howe'er aspirants strive,
"O'er midnight dip of sperm or tallow gleam.
   "So, mayhap, some sense her tales may have at base,
"In case of which well she deserves of us—
"A judgment revised at least, with frank avowal all
"That much misjudg'd was she, her field of play miscalled,
"Hence to be known as the Wise Goddess' Sphere."
   Then Lincoln quizzical, with eyes strangely alight:
   "If she be truthful then, and not a goddess false
"Assured my future is and I o'er land shall rule
"And do some needful things to strength our common house
"That calls for handiwork lest roof and walls collapse

"Thro' that black wedge, malign as raven-croak,—
"Thanks to Tyrant King,—as early annals show—
"Deep in our stately prop, the bane of our roof-tree,
"Which, like a festering sore, with angry flesh and proud,
"Doth breed disquiet e'er with sure dissensions harsh,
"Promotive e'er of Caste, debasing moral sense
"And violating that for which our forebears fought,—
"The Liberty of Man, the right divine to live
"And move as free as air; winning fruits of toil
"For use of him and his with none to say him nay,
"Whate'er he might elect that in his province is,
"For weal or woe of him and those for whom he strives.
"It cannot be that this, our Freedom won so hard,
"Shall e'er be marr'd by moans sad on our ears that fall
"And deeply pierce, and heart and conscience sear,
"And tell us day by day what hypocrites we be
"Parading Freedom's joys and living thus a lie;
"And, I have fancies had that all in season due
"The hand of God, in His appointed way,
"Will fall with heaviness upon this Thing of shame
"And fearful reck'ning make, unless we wake betimes
"And right the monstrous wrong that stains our Nation's name.
    "Likewise have I had thought that I some humble part
"In such high task might have—the salvage of a race
"That groans 'neath lash, and toils thro' blood and tears
"With ne'er a ray of light to lift its heart in hope,
"But seeing day by day its lov'd ones dragg'd away,
"The babe from mother torn, the damsel from the hut
"Where doting elders joy'd to see the maiden bloom,—
"The hope and stay of age,—she reft from them despite
"The grief and wailings deep, as lamb torn from its dam,
" 'Midst plaintive bleatings there that o'er the field resound
"And touch the hearts of all whose wakeful ears do hear."
    As he ceased to speak she for a moment lay
Thoughtful, motionless, as one in spell profound,
Then looking in his face, 'roused intellect there marked,
With arch expression and merriment in eye,
Commented thus in tone that to him full pleasing was:
    "We have surely dealt with high and weighty things,
"Bringing the world, so speaking, hither to our feet:

"And when we pause and think that they upon whose deeds we dwell
"Have long since pass'd, those millions in the range
"Of our own consciousness, how slight a thing doth seem
"That death which many fear:—the spacious pathway hence
"O'er which we all are bound, some early and some late,
"In harmony with law, by the All-wise decreed!—
"Motion eternal set, e'en as our planet moves
"Thro' further realms of space, with all the firmament
"Borne with it,—not less bright that it doth speed along
"E'er onward to some bourne e'en from world's wisest hid.
  "We live and pass in shoals, leaving empty shells,
"To strew Life's shores whilst others take our place.
"They too, in brief, to pass e'en as their forebears did,—
"The swarms that till'd before and opened up the way
"In that New World for us and those who after come—
"Endless procession of life manifest and life invisible—
"As ship emerging safe in port from wat'ry world of mist
"That screens from view long line of vessels in her wake,          [trust
"In which one Mighty Hand doth move us all, in whose high lead we
"E'en as in mortal things, same faith reflecting, trust we our leaders
"And the doings of those gone, commingled with our own,          [here:
"Time's hand, mosaic-like, in sequence lays on base impalpable
"And yield behold!—is History, alluring e'er to us
"Of current time, because in calm perspective shown
"The acts of minds that passed before, all free from passion gauged,
"To make us wise in light of such if we do view aright."

# VII

*Lincoln, after leaving the couch of his intended bride, takes a long walk, during which he falls into a strange trance, a result of his morbid state of mind and fancies himself on the far-off Atlantic coast in the early time of the first arrival of the Puritans. He walks with them along the strand of the strange new land and his heart is touched on beholding them at frequent intervals, shade their eyes with a hand and gaze far seaward toward the land they left as if hoping to catch a glimpse of its shore. He leads them away from the beach, impressed by their prim simplicity of dress and sober demeanor, but is presently astonished to hear sounds of laughter and glee, and turning finds to his surprise that the quiet, solemn throng has vanished and in their place is a multitude of blacks, following his steps and singing hosannas as if some joyous event, long foretold, had come to pass.*

Then signs of weariness on count'nance fair, disclosed,
When stoop'd fond lover low with eyes and face alight
And kiss'd the drooping lids, then straight'ning in his chair,
With reach of ling'ring hand to there on pillow rest
In spell of calm and peace, and stroke the shining hair
In soothing fond caress, until anon the eyes
Did gently close, and curving lashes lay
Unstirring, and then he knew she slept;
And rising noiselessly he stole away for solitary stride
Adown the silent road thro' meagre town that led
Upon whose streets he car'd not kindly ones to face,
Who knew his woe, and whose respectful looks,
Not less than halting speech, would be as poignant darts,
Confirming in his heart that fear of loss to be.
   Far did he stalk past lanes and homesteads new
With garish clearings shown and flare of brushwood fires,
From countless piles ascending, with pungent odors rife
The fresh spring air there lading, with tang infectious charged,
As curling smoke swirled up and wove strange fantasies
Mimeing the farther clouds, o'erarched by languid sky
'Neath which toiled men and beasts as e'er in past have toiled
Wild lands to so subdue, plow and axe in grip
As sturdy limbs did guide or swing in woodman's ply,
As gladly they wrought for no taskmaster's dole

But for themselves and theirs with all the likely fruits
The fertile soil would yield, the willing price there paid,
Self-sacrifice and toil for few initial years,
Of luxuries much depriving for boon of larger, fuller life
Of later time, and hence, o'er expectation high
Finding hardest task in heart's elation light.
    All these he passed, rude wooden bowers reared
By those new-come, o'er long and varied ways,
Wherein he e'er was welcome; but wishing naught save leave
All undisturbed to be he walked with e'er avoiding eye
In meditation deep o'er well-springs touched by her
In recent converse, source of things so vast
Great thoughts did throng and, overflowing, filled
To full his consciousness, rend'ring self as naught;
Whilst moving thro' his being, all autonomous,
In wide kingdom of unchained Fancy came
A host of images,—impalpable, adrift,—
Of things achieved by others and of things to be,
In which he might have share and mayhap own a name
To hail the unborn years in honor thence to stand
'Mongst men revered, helpful to Age and kind
In their life-day, and so to all who after came.
    And meditating thus, 'midst pressing memories
Dream-like he plodded on in strange obliviousness
Of burden'd present, fraught with such meanings drear,
And seemed to walk with those of faint and far-off coast
Down ghost-like stretch of sands o'ercast by arching blue
With somber wat'ry waste, and foam, and e'er unending break
Of sea 'gainst shore in one long reach forlorn,
Holding enwrapt in fold of its gray mystery
Vast hidden destiny of New World there born;
Fancying as he moved with mind trance-like and vague
In weird and groping spell, that he had voyaged far
To that bleak shore, an ache within his breast,
O'er sense of some great loss, to him yet undefined,
As moved 'mongst others there and gently helped along
The tott'ring steps of old and frail in garb of Puritan,
Noting staid, set ways, and how they ever clung
In habitations prim, hard by the lonely beach,
And in their march would turn and wistfully there gaze,

Rigid and still, hand o'er eyes, in all too futile strain
Far seaward, and his heart was touched.
  And in his fancy, all so real, seemed a mingling there
Of walls and roofs e'en strangely like, as if New Salem Town
Had been transplanted; then the fleeting thought
Did come, that as were they aback in misty time
On that dim coast, so wert they on far frontier—
Each in his time and plight to same experience know
In sense of newness, with privations sure in wake,
Yet e'er brave hearts the hardest lot to overcome,
And make earth's wastes to bloom and in abundance yield
Of its rich store for weal of man and creature-kind.
  Making distinctions thus he thought he walked with them,
Those pallid, lean of visage with eyes and mien devout,
Who seem'd uplifted all, and in cheer to greet him well
And hold to him as those decrepit cling to nearest prop
And welcome there his coming, as of advent foreknown
And with pent-joy, long waited,—the whole dim throng in march
With him in lead, o'er shelving shore, e'er washed by phantom sea
Empty of sail or hull e'en as an ocean dead—
For, when wast barque or sign of sea-craft known there
Ere came those wanderers o'er?—they who didst now attend
With faces turned henceforth toward beck'ning inland reach
Of field and forest,—features relaxt and glad,
And from them mirth and joy,—which did not beseem the Puritan—
As e'er fulfillment of some boon e'en long foretold and hoped.
  Then, in his dream, he turn'd, all curious, and looked
To find, with keen surprise, the picture changed,—
Those who first did greet all vanished,—the slim ascetics pale,—
Leaving in their stead a throng with faces black
Who danced and wept for gladness, and fell each on other's necks,
And laugh'd and shouted in medley of wild glee
And sang hosannas weird, and joined their happy hands,
Whilst elders there, packs on backs and helpful staffs, did beam,
And mothers with their babes press'd on with shining looks,
All hurrying in wake of him as one who steadfast led
Unto some joyous goal,—a wild and 'wildering scene,—
Tumult so stressful the o'erwrought dreamer woke
To find, amaz'd—as by enchanter's wand—
The fantasy dissolving,—and looking—behold! the sun was low,

His golden wings outflung o'er peaceful western sky
And mellow light diffused o'er vast expanse of plain.
   Then, with self-reproach for needless absence long
His steps he turned and back more swiftly strode,
Her refresh'd from sleep to find and others at her couch,
Mother and sister, with nourishment scarce touched,
Yet, with eyes alight and bloom upon her cheeks
As if heart-joy anew were hers which, in its fullness, sought
Outlet to him that he with her might share.
   As they, the others, then, with kindly greeting passed
From presence there and left the two alone.
He stooping, kiss'd, and fondly strok'd her cheeks,
And sitting down, his hand upon her brow
Look'd the query her speaking eyes didst raise.

# VIII

*She also had a strange dream in which it appeared Washington had not died but lived in deep seclusion in a beautiful mountain-girded home in a remote part of Virginia, to which she made a pilgrimage and was, after certain signs of disquiet from the object of her quest, received kindly upon her modest explanation of her purpose in coming from the great outer world. Then follows a surprising journey, as Washington sets out with her and visits the cities and towns of the future, with all the wondrous improvements and, most surprising of all, points out monuments, statues and busts to the memory of Lincoln.*

"I see the question on your face," she said
"And you will hear with pleasure of my tour
"Thro' mazes of delight and fraught with wondrous things,—
"The strangest ever heard!—the most marvelous!
  "I have had in truth a moving, vivid dream—
"Which yet seems not a dream, so truly real it was—
"That took me o'er throng'd ways of all the glorious land
"Of which we lately talk'd, and, most singular of all
"My guide was he, our Greatest, the one beyond compare,
"First in our hearts whose genius shines thro' time,
"Whom all thought dead,—a vast delusion, seeming;
"He had not died but here alive and well
"Was still himself, and when I found it so—
"From hazy dream awak'd, as seem'd, that had my sense misled—
"I thought there stole, scarce noticed, within my being tense
"The dawn of wonder e'er the vast deceit
"That made parade of all pertaining things
"That Greatness knows when it doth close its day;—
"Deceit so artful there as made similitude,
"In ev'ry shade and touch, with actuality;—        [acts—
"First, the cause of illness,—symptoms grave—the summoned doctor's
"Outside commotion—the nearing end—last words—the closing scene
      of all—
"The burial—the flood of eulogies—the moral from his life-work drawn!
  "All these had seem'd to flit thro' previous dream that he was dead
" 'Till undeceived by dream that showed him still in life
"When all perfection of former dream's deception shone,

52

"O'er which methought I marvelled much that a mere dream
"Should so particularize the things that be in truth, [dream,
"And my awakening,—if I may so term the lapse,—to that great
"Did all more make me glad that what I had believed were such
"Was but fantasy, which brought mind and heart to all more appreciate
"The Fraud's unmasking, e'en so subtly framed;
"And swift did crystalize resolve to wakeful self repay
"By instant homage to the living Great, revered,
"Rendered in ardor more intense by reason of the shock
"The dream that he was dead did so impose on me;—
"All films of fancy of disordered brain,
"Quite reverse of truth, delusion most complete
"So far as held, which I might with cause resent
"And full condemn, yet so glad was I
"That he did live, no wish had I to quarrel
"With vision false. He lived! the Earth did hold him still!
"That was enough! I did not stay my feet
"But light as air at once set on my pilgrimage.
    "He lived! he lived! but far in middle-land,
"From jar of world remote,—and stir of pressing throngs,—
"Yet his Virginia still, in deep seclusion drawn
"In realm of tints and haze where misty mountains show
"Far o'er a landscape fair, their crests upswelling high
"In sea of ether vast, whose filmy breath descends
"And bathes the bulky forms, aspiring there to pierce
"The bounds of azure world which thus their heads enmesh
"In rare contrasting hues as sunlight o'er them plays
"And lends a splendor e'en to all that intervenes,—
"Entrancing land which to those aweary brings
"The boon of peace where hearts may pine no more.
    "So on I sped o'er radiant miles that lay
"Invitingly twixt me and object of my quest.
"And there were levels wide, and groves of mighty oaks
"Old as the gnarled and wen'd whose shades the Druids knew,
"With kingly spread of branch, and verdant turf beneath,
"Grand as the haunts of eld when ancient Briton stalked
"And Priest's and Priestess' rites his rugged spirit swayed;—
"Great boles, o'er heads of which had hoary centuries sped,
"Twixt which bright sunlight play'd e'en as in misty time
"When antlered stag flashed by with docile herd in wake

"And man and beast, full bold, wild life of Forest shared.
   "Where dark green fields did show and sparkling streamlets were
"Dim 'neath o'erhanging boughs, then bright in stretch of light,
"With yellow, sandy shoals, that golden glimmer wore,
"There led a road,—mysterious, strange, e'en like a speaking thing,—
"Such objects mem'ry glimps'd, of seeming scenes gone by,—
"Familiar, yet unplaced, harking back to youthful days,
"Where e'er dear mem'ries lie, at will to come and go,—
"With banks now low, now high, by lofty trees o'erhung
"Whose mighty roots, exposed at times, and out-protruding far,
"Queer fret-work made,—all Nature's vagaries
"Their forms betraying, bordered by a land scarce real—
"To sense so seeming—that all in deepest silence lay,—
"A stillness that oppressed,—no stir of bird nor man nor beast
"Nor of wing'd insect tribe;—a world of rest profound,—
"Nor sign of trav'ller there save I who breathed that air;—
"A land enwrapt in sleep, as seem'd, yet showing tendence strict
"As if by unseen hands, place 'neath Enchantment spell,
"All fit, methought, and full significant,
"Environment of Mystic Seat that so much Greatness held;
"And soon within my view in easy reach there shone
"A pillared home, with lattice-pale, and ample grounds around.
   "White wall'd it was, and pleasing,—as shell-enameled set in green—
"With box-wood squares and bordered walks and blooming plant and
"And many a tree with rip'ning fruit of colors manifold,      [shrub
"And floral beds with fragrant blooms of varied scents and hues—
"Bewild'ring scenes of charm and beauty,—from outer road approached
"By broad and pebbly way, with lordly trees aligned
"Whose ancient trunks and wide o'erhanging boughs
"A natural trellis made and screened the brilliant light
"From o'erhead that fell, unto more softened rays.
   "How I that Seat did find I ne'er made pause to know;
"Suffice that I was there, e'en as the Homing flies,
"When once released, unerring to its loft
"Tho' leagues, a thousand 'twixt, may intervene.
   "And there, as I drew nigh, on broad verandah-seat
"Where shelt'ring leaves of sweet vines flowering climbed,
"And beds of jasmine, phlox and bright verbenas were,
"Sate he, embodiment of Greatness, as our minds conceive
"To us, his kind, so seeming; with that lofty nature shown

"In looks and bearing; nor touch of pride nor affectation there—
"A nature too great for aught dissembling,—truth personified—
"With dignity that did with noble mind comport,
"As one above all stratas of self-int'rest raised,
"Who aim'd for good of man with undiluted wish,
"Finding reward alone in joy o'er service to his kind—
"An ideal that showed his soul, leaving naught in look or mien
"There wanting,—the form, the face, the bearing, all
"In millions of hearts enshrined, here on earth before my eyes!
　"He sat with look of meditation and scarce seemed
"To notice me save by simple nod and motion of his hand
"To nearby seat;—no word of greeting, as tho' used to those
"Who came to pay their homage; and I had feeling then
"That he was wearied and would like their visits less,
"With fleeting thought that,—as shown in false dream—supposed,—
"He would speechless be, as in last sleep in calm Mount Vernon's shade,
"For all the spoken welcome he would tender me.
　"Then, I know not how it came that I his nature touched;
"Began I there my speech and heart's fullness free outpoured,
"Dwelling on words and deeds, not less than soul and mind
"That had so shaped the lives of us, given his land a Creed
"That e'er our anchor is in time of storm and stress,
"Born of sophistries that live their little hour
"To fall before the might of his example great.
　"And, too, I told him there how mind of ev'ry school-child glowed
"In young unfoldment, o'er his acts,—how as a Beacon he
"Before their eyes e'er loomed whilst love of country thrilled
"Young hearts and souls, and turned their thoughts upon
"The boon conferred by him, and those, his great compeers,
"Winning way for us in this New World to live
"Free as the blessed air, mindful of others' rights,
"With laws humane and just, the armor of our weal.
　"Thus I did pay my homage, glad that yet on earth he lived [believe
"To hear my words and not, as false dream—supposed—had made me

# IX

*In her dream Washington takes her on a journey to the Eastern cities where she beholds the wonders of the future, including various statues and monuments to the memory of Lincoln over which she marvels much; and, presently coming to a statue, bearing his face, set in medallion, she notes its care-worn look and bursts into tears. At one of the monuments a group of blacks are gathered paying homage to the subject.*

"When I had ceased, again he motioned me to sit,
"Then looking at me with grave and kindly eyes
"That seem'd to hold all things, Past, Present and to come,—
"Such wisdom of expression and calm benignity withal;—
"But I chose to stand, an attitude more fit
"In presence of such Greatness, and slowly shook my head.
  "He read my mind, no doubt, then came a thing unlooked,—
"Most wonderful of all! as if he those, my yearnings, knew;—
"Unbending he uprose and gently took my hand
"And led the way thro' stately hall into a maze whereof
"Gray mist enshrouded, and I seemed somehow to know
"That other hands than Man's environed him and set
"His destiny apart as guardian of the land
"By him through years of hardship won,—those daring souls he led
"With bleeding feet through winter's rigors harsh,
"Their stains in blotches red so piteously to mark
"The jagged rocks outthrust, and dye the rivulets,
"With Schuylkill's flood to merge, enshrined historic stream
"Upon which oft his sad grave eyes did gaze
"As thoughts didst rise of his Potomac loved
"And happy days on that, his native shore,
"And then contrast with such the troubles thick
"That so did crowd upon him—he the hope and stay
"Of young tott'ring Nation's weal.  And then in mind indeed—
"Like picture flash that sheen of glass or water gives—
"The storied heights and vale, that deep heart-mem'ries hold
"Did rise impressive, with inseperably there joined
"His name and deeds,—he, high Warder e'er to be

"Of lands dominion wide,—though of it no more
"In visual sense, but as one removed,
"And seated far apace wherefrom undying light—
"As lamp the vestal virgins kept—of wisdom and high name
"Doth way illume for Patriot Helmsman thro' all time to come
"And keep thereby steadfast and true the State's imposing ship
"Whate'er the turmoil of Great World at large might be.
   "These thoughts I had as he did walk with me.
   "And as he led the winding way was dim
"Until, to sudden turn came we and I beheld far down the haze
"A city set with stars—so seeming—and, the walk, more clear,
"Downward we went, taking straight and easy course
"Toward shining lure.  On level earth again,
"We onward pressed and soon a gorgeous way
"Before our eyes did ope and all its stretch was bright,—
"Pavements alive with fleeting forms, each brushing other brisk
"As to and fro sped they, ten times ten thousand varying shades
"Of looks and ways revealed.  Onward yet moved we,
"In swirling vital stream past structures grand, ornate,          [light,
"By grace of Craftsman's art their charm, all bright with bursts of
"A dizzy, 'wild'ring sight, until, betimes we reached
"A plat of Nature's own,—rural world in miniature,—
"Fair patch of green, offset from whirring, busy, street,—
"To aching eyes refreshing,—where gushing fountain played,
"Its spray glad coolness show'ring, and near, a spacious mound,
"From which in tow'ring grandeur rose a stately monument
"Of whitest marble pure, and—wonder on wonders piled!
"On base a wrought medallion, decked with circling, chiseled wreath
"In which a face did show and there beneath, a name—
"The face and name of you, clear as the light around that shone!
"Not, not, the face that now before me is
"But more mature, and bearded,—a face o'er which the years had crept,
"Yet eyes, and nose and head and other features same;
"And signs of stress did show upon the wrinkled brow
"As if much thought and care had ploughed their furrows there;
"And eyes were set and sad, seeing not with out-sent look
"But holding deep to inner vision as tho' the storm had passed
"And sight of mind did view the crucial trials now o'er,
"With you content, relieved, to there react in peace
"And inward contemplation too profound for words—

"A face so thoughtful, sad, that my heart was touched
"And scalding tears methought did damp and burn my cheeks.
    "Our place resumed in moving tide, soon came we afront
"A column'd sculptured pile that lorded o'er the rest,
"With plaza green wherefrom a statue rose in bronze;
"Life size, on metal base it was, a shapely pedestal,        [and form
"Embossed with shield and wrought laurel-wreath, whilst head and face
"Were you!—with name in letters bright displayed,
"As if some careful hand with daily task entrust
"The work as honor prized, and e'en gave extra touch
"To make the lett'ring shine and thus keep shining e'er the name;
"And in right hand, half raised, a metal scroll
"As there denoting act of mark with which your life was linked,
"Whilst near about impressive statue-base,
"Respectful, awe-struck, with heads uncovered stood
"A group of blacks, gazing with full and rev'rent eyes
"Your face and form upon, as viewing there an object worshipful.
    "Then we pressed on, leaving the town behind,
"Thro' labyrinthian way, for a long space, it seemed,
" 'Till from a height that to us vantage gave
"A shore appeared and far adown its reach,
"Like a bright moon that peers above a cloud,
"A city lay 'neath cold and crystal sky,—
"Prospect fair as that o'er cool New Foundland's wastes
"Whereon gaze they, the fisher-folk, on bright September day,—
"With smoke and steam thro' vents by thousands sent
"Beyond the roofs that myriads sheltered there;
"Some streets seen circling sharp, as tire round the wheel.
    "In area wide,—that thronging hive of men,—
"Outspread from water's edge where wharves a plenty showed
"While num'rous craft the bounding waves skimm'd o'er,
"Their sails sunlit and bright as up and down they fared
"O'er heaving breast of that long wane of coast."

# X

*She describes their advent in the "City of the Puritans" and the throngs on the streets. It is Memorial Day, and, following the throngs she and her illustrious guide reach Bunker Hill, and visit the famous Boston Commons and behold, as they pass, other monuments and busts to the memory of Lincoln. They next visit New York, the throngs and activities of whose streets are described.*

"Soon we were there in proud and noted Seat
"By Puritan upreared, the fixt resplendent star
"In galaxy of those, land's early Cities great;
"Scene of my longings, near whose centre rose
"The hill of Bunker's name, to patriot-heart endeared,
"Within brief hail of Lexington and Concord, famed—
"Names ne'er to be forgot whilst men love Liberty.

  "And thro' the streets, by moving masses thronged,
"We took our course, afloat in human tide
"That endless seemed until a break,—behold!
"An open space, and circling round we saw
"A spacious park, the walks with thousands dense,
"As 'twere some gala day, and many bore bright wreaths
"And floral off'rings, old and young, and all intent
"On thing in view,—likewise a statue large
"With plenteous garlands hung,—memorial fair, to you!
"Your face, your form, your name in shining letters clear
"E'en as those that late our eyes beheld.

  "And as the throngs, slow-moving, dense to other scenes repaired
" 'Twas e'er the same;—in wall'd nich, plaza and plat of green
"Where'er did public flock memorial was,—statue, bust, or monument,
"All, all to you; and oft your name in golden letters showed
"E'en as that of him, seen in supposed deluding dream.

  "Once more pressed we in hazy labyrinth
"And came anon to place where ears and eyes were dazed
"By wondrous sights and sounds,—a ne'er ending Babel wild
"The brain that set awhirl, as he who notes swift-moving wheel
"With steadfast gaze and finds suspended sense beneath its spell;—
"Such sounds and sights in space of Earth all new

"Did mark a city of pretentions and of greatness far
" 'Yond those we left.  Hedg'd twixt two rivers wide—
"Arms there of briny sea, and by the sea itself—
"Where ocean-flood an island made—it long had held chief name
" 'Mongst marts of trade and barter, where wharves of vast extent did
"And ships of every clime, from world-wide waters come,         [show
"To fetch and carry.  And, e'er moving craft on those deep rivers
            screamed,                                           [wild,
"Or, with deep bellow roar'd, with clang of bells and voices raucous,
"And ne'er the din did cease as up and down they sped
"Large and small—ev'ry size and form displayed,
"Crowding wat'ry space as if from ends of earth came they
"And naught in motion was save what did swim or float
"With plentious sail displayed, yet more of smoke and fire,
"Thousands of puffing, clanging demons loosed, the rivers there to fret,
"Keeping so stunn'd the ears 'twere almost madness sheer
"To try to think or talk save in terms of wonderment.
    "Ent'ring the town 'midst all the din, and once again engulfed
"In surging human tide, we floated o'er the course,
"Main art'ry there, of surcharg'd, pressured net of ways,
"For distance long and e'er same scene beheld,—
"Bedlam broke loose and those outflown here darting swift about,
"With jarring clang and crossing-men high-keyed
"To tension ne'er relaxt,—on edge unceasingly,—
"To stem the traffic brisk, and curb the 'wildering pace
"Of human streams that swirl'd and eddied with unabating flow.
    "As one who travels far o'er hot and dusty way
"And finds relief at last in cool and shady glen
"So we, our course diverting, and meeting welcome sight
"Of tall cool trees with lake and shrubb'ry nigh,
"And walks and drives and varied scenic nooks,
"Proclaiming spacious park; and, floating with the stream,
"That far ahead in even volume showed,
"Came at length to halt, as others in our lead,
"To view again, in grand impressive form,
"A statue there of you, in dignity enthroned.
    "Next we repaired to that famed old city, known
"To Patriot-heart by ev'ry word synonymous
"With what our hearts do cherish,—Cradle of Liberty,—
"Of Nation's Independence proud and honored Seat,—

"She, whose noted Bell on glorious day proclaimed
"Unto earth's ends a glad free Nation born.
  "And there as elsewhere—on ev'ry hand the same—
"Memorial piles, statues, busts, all in your honor shone!
"And in golden letters here and there where'er the eye did turn—
"Institutions rich, edifice, and Home, for varied uses reared,—
"And streets, driveways and great boulevards
"All, all, did e'er commemorate the magic Lincoln name.
  "And, too, in all our journeyings, where'er the Changers were,
"In marts of commerce brisk, in shop or booth or gayly decked bazaar
"There shone the Lincoln face on sterling coin, bank-note and copper
"Profusely stamped as e'er visage was of him of Rome          [mite
"Of whose didst Savior of the world direct strict rend'ring up;
"And so, on stamps likewise, and medals, trinkets, and varied charms
"Same likeness showing, as one of cherished name          [ornate,
"To all endeared, both high and low alike,
"And e'er to be honored,—crowned with undying glory bright.
  "Yet, o'er all else a mightier tribute shone,
"An e'er enduring boon, to use of man decreed
"As Panorama great before our gaze revealed,—
"Vast face of Continent from end to end in view,
"Configurations all and varied features clear,
"With seas and lakes, and mountains high, and far-extended plains,—
"A sight so striking large, as brought staid sense to reel,—
"New World outspread before calm Contemplation's eye—
"Immensity in leash that staggered Vision's poise,—
"With cities, towns and farmsteads green, in countless myriads shown,
"Whilst o'er the mighty reach, from ocean shore to ocean shore again,
"O'er miles by thousands gauged, a broad and whited way,
"On spell-bound eyes did break as land's extremes it joined;
"Thro' States by scores e'er coursing, impressive, serpentinian, grand,
"O'er Appalachian heights, and central plain and Rocky range in turn
"To shining land aglow that broad Pacific greets;—
"A Highway superb, 'yond far what Past did know, devise or dream,—
"A thousand Appian Ways, by others still prolonged,
"Its length excelling, as o'er rivers wide and lofty mountain-range,
"And vale and plain, it held its lordly way,
"Riding majestically, e'en as the wind that sweeps
"O'er mount and hollow, upland, and prairie wide,
"With rise and fall, as fixt gradations were,

"Sheafing up earth-space, annihilating bounds
"Divisional and marked,—annulling lines of East and West
"As gleaming mile-posts told o'er stretch of surfaced polished length,
"A span prodigious wrought, o'er which bright Sol aweary grew
"At e'er persistent sight, and drooped in sheer futility,
"Closing his orb in sleep, e'en as we humans do,
"Sinking low to rest e'er came the terminus
"Of vasty whole in one full solar day.
"And, as we gazed a golden mist arose
"And tinted broad white band with ornate tracery
"In which wast woven there in shining letters large,
"Outstanding clear, in all-compelling view,
"The name of you, and, in this sensed we, with start
"The title designate of what our eyes beheld,—
"The mighty ligament that binds a hemisphere.
    "Then I recall'd in vision, the dream that held my guide as dead—
"Strange how we dream of dreams and e'en marvel o'er it in our
            dreams—
"And, remembering statues, busts, and monuments to him, as seen
"In that suppos'd delusive spell, did ponder how it were with him
"When he should pass in truth; and then there flashed the thought
"That he would never die, but, in a sort of twilight-zone
"Would live his years through all eternity,
"While those, the rest, would go e'en as now we pass;
"And I thought it pity then that he could ne'er depart
"And have memorials such as my dream had shown of you.
"Yet,—strange contradiction!—I did not think of you as dead
"But 'mongst the living still, e'en when I those memorials saw,
"And I found me wishing in my dream the while
"That he might pass, e'en as we mortals do,
"Since else, he left alone, would be in world so far progressed
"From that in early touch, that he would be, as seem'd to me,
"As a lost child on some strange crowded pier,          [thenceforth,
"From parents, sisters and brothers parted, and there, yawning deep,
"The sundered heart and those loving and so lov'd, between,
"The awful barrier of a wide deep sea,
"He thence to wear his life away and never know them more.
    "With this, the theme enlarging, came the rasping thought—
"Disquieting and drear—that for any one of us
"Who lingers here, outliving all the friends of youth,—

"Those beings dear round which our heart's affections cling,—
"How cold the world must seem and with what longings deep
"To go the way of those so lov'd, must lone survivor feel!
"For, lives do pass in vast platoons and those left far in wake
"Do lag as stragglers, stumbling blindly on,
"Or striving to hold their pace with those who know them not
"And look upon them strangely, as if questioning
"Why they were left, with drear suggestion back of all
"That space is grudg'd whereon they hold by rushing, thronging ones
"With glowing youth and thoughts and bounding aspirations high,
"Who taste life's sweets ere experience full the mind doth ope
"To show a vaster world where endless splendors lie
"Of which this life is faint reflex; and those who go before
"Emerge in realm beyond and new dawning find
"That wondrously their state and those they leave behind      [old,
"Doth then transpose, and they are young, whilst those on earth are
"Like the new shoot that from fertile garden springs,
"Leaving stalk behind, soon to wither and decay.

    "So, coming back again to thought which made me reason thus
"I felt opprest, that he, my lofty Guide, who had so favored me,
"Were fated e'er on earth to bide and not to pass as others do
"But far removed in misty land remote
"Must live and yet not live, for all men heard or saw of him
"In heyday of world-life,—he so far away.

    "Thus, torturings in my mind,—or fancy, which e'er it be—
"Deeply vext I felt and woke to find my mother and my sister here—
"To say that I was talking and tossing in my sleep,—
"And realized with something of a shock, 'tis true,
"That Washington was dead, and what I dreamt I'd dreamed
"Was truth, and then I felt relieved to know
"That after all he had his monuments, statues and busts
"As were his due, and thus my burden passed.

    "So I have had my journey and with rapt joy have seen
"Those rare glad places o'er which my heart had yearned,—
"Tho' chang'd and far progress'd—with things of future blent,
"And, all hailing name of you, dream-picture strange 'tis true
"Yet one I believe fortelling that which is to be."
    As she ceased her eyes did brightly beam
Her love upon him, and he, stooping, caught
Her to his breast and there did hold her close

In long embrace, then releasing her he drew
Her pillow nearer, and with gentle hand did ease
Her head upon it, and look'd at her with no will for speech.
  Watching him with eyes of merriment she silent lay
Until his pause, prolonged, did prompt her voice again to speak:
  "Have you no word," she asked, half in plaintiveness
"For my wondrous dream?—No thanks for what it brought?
"Those monuments, statues and the busts, as well
"Are worth a simple 'Thank you' at least,
"And those golden-letter liberties taken with your name,
"What say you, Sir, of that—Nothing at all?"

# XI

*Lincoln quizzically comments on the memorials reared in his honor as seen by her in her dream, declaring she has appropriated the busts, statues and monuments erected to the memory of Washington to the credit of himself and playfully accuses her of grand larceny. Her prophetic reply. She tells him of the wonders seen in her dream-journey. The telegraph, telephone, trolley and airplane described. He then relates his dream which recalls a strange incident when she was away at school and had her fortune told.*

Then with quaint humor, alight in face and eye
Which brought a wondrous change and made her love him more,—
A face transfigured as his spirit glowed—
He backward leaned, raised arms and clasping hands behind his head
Regarded her with look of mock gravity and said:
  "These honors with which you load me are too much
"And I might well be silent o'er unexpected lift
"From dark obscurity to light of dazzling fame;
"But, as the man who has another's goods,
"Knowing he came not by them honestly and fair
"I feel embarrassment that tells me it were best
"To hold my tongue.  Those statues, busts and monuments
"Which you describe, were property of your noble guide
"And you, having me in mind, and wishing for my weal,
"Did regularly appropriate them, a crime I think they call
"Grand Larceny, being of such large degree.
"I am o'erwhelmed by such sacrifice upon your part."
  Then she, half-pouting:  "Now you laugh at me
"And would make it seem that I no feeling had
"Of due respect for him who so honored me
"By taking me through all the glorious round
"Of those noted places o'er which I had so longed
"And which before my eyes I still can see
"With all their moving busy throngs and ways."
  "I think," Lincoln rejoined, still the same seriousness assuming,
"That to other offense you also are answerable for forgery,—
"Transferring those memorials from him to me
"And even affixing my name where his had been."

Upon her pillow then she shook her head
And looked at him half reproachfully:
"You may laugh," she said, "but Sir, to me
"Those memorials have a meaning that augurs more
"Than I can frame in words.  I think a future great
"For you was in that dream enwrapt; and I do believe
"That he, my glorious guide, was leading me thro' days
"That are to be; for, I saw many wondrous things
"Not to be seen on all the earth to-day; things indescribable
"Whereby people talked o'er strings of wire, outspread o'er the land
"In endless lines on poles that girded East and West
"And North and South, and e'en ran 'neath the ocean's waves
"To olden World, o'er which went messages both to and from
"By thousands during night and day.
"And thro' the streets ran cars and vehicles unique,
"Propelled by means unseen, at smooth and rapid rate;
"And women sat in shops—and men also as seen—
"With sewing work done swiftly, no more by toilsome hand
"But by strange machines, by light foot-power run.
  "But strangest of all, high circling overhead
"Were bird-like objects huge, with mighty wings outspread
"And men were guiding them, thousands of feet in air
"With wondrous chugging noise that broke on ears below,
"As if earth not alone did Man's dominion claim
"But realm of vasty space above, as well."
  Then Lincoln serious o'er new unfoldments sat
With mind abstracted, with introspective look
In eyes that gazed her way tho' unseeing, as if thro' space afar
'Yond curtain'd years he saw the wonders which her fancy framed;
Then coming to himself, with shift of posture said:
  "The germs of hope and dregs of fear do rise in dreams
"To gladden or depress us, which e'er the case may be.
"I, too, have had my dream, a walking, waking vision sent,    [sheep.
"E'en as we read of those of old who walked lone fields and tended
"Myself walk'd thro' the misty days with somber Puritans,
"In mien and ways most real, environment the same;
"And me they welcomed heartsomely, and crowded there around
"As if I bore some message, and hemm'd me all about
" 'Till I must lead them forth, from the wet strand away
"And onward with faces fixt to course of setting sun,

"As if Land's destiny there lay and not by wave-wash'd shore;
"And then, quick shift of scene, the thing was wholly changed.
"Instead of Puritans of quiet, decorous ways,
"I found myself at head of gleeful throng of blacks,—
"Women, children, men—mothers with babes at breast,—
"Gray age with tott'ring steps, and tender infancy,
"All merged in that great horde, with tears, laughter and dancing there
"Like a full Bedlam loos'd,—and then I from walking trance awoke
"And felt much self-reproach that I so long had been from you."
    Wide-eyed she looked at him, surprise writ on her face,
Her parted lips and breath indrawn, denoting int'rest tense
As if to her the dream held meaning all unthought by him,—
Some cryptic saying deep that mind oft ponders o'er
And gropes for light and then desists only to try again
Yet ever balk'd until anon there flashes forth the key
And full-revealed, the hidden truth, with startling vividness.
And, in the pause that held him questioning,
She found her voice and in wond'ring accents said:
    "What time I was away there in the rising classic town
"In that much vaunted school with pleasant student-mates
"A certain few of us would ramble far afoot
"To breathe the open air and feast on Nature's joys as well;
"A merry girlish set whose laugh was tonic, pure,—
"And as we walked one day deep in an oaken wood
"There glimmered down the way a brilliant roadside mound
"As of an image carv'd in sitting posture grave,
"Or life-size form of clay, wrought by some Aztec hand,
"Enriched with scarlet dye, that shimmered thro' the trees;
"And as we curious mov'd, our eager eyes intent,
"The shape revealed itself,—a turban'd, mantled one,
"A dame with swarthy face dressed all in brightest red
"With trinkets a plenty deck'd, on hands and ears and breast;
"With dark compelling eyes that peered thro' mystery,
"Who, as we came, held out to us her hand,
"Brown as the acorn-shell, from sun of many climes,—
"And crav'd a trifle, as we willed, to have our future read,
"Which straight our fancy caught and we there reckoned up
"Such coin as we possessed and made compact with her
"Our palms to read and faithful version give.
    "So up we step in line, I holding last of all,

"And when my turn was come and I reached out my hand
"She glanced and straightened quick and lifted high her head,
"Gave one grand bow as if she saw afar
"A throne reserved for me and I in regal robe,
"And said with voice intoned that all did deeply thrill:
  "It is your lot to be to more than King endeared;
"The bride to be of one whose name shall shine
"When Kings and Potentates of earth shall all forgotten be.
"Not his the pomp and glamour of the regal line
"But one more mighty still, whose hand shall duly strike
"And rive the fetters harsh that pinch and gall the flesh
"Of enslaved millions, and win a glory that his name shall crown
"Thro' untold ages of the time to be."
  "She look'd then sadly at me—such steadfast, penetrating look—
"And pressed my hand and murmured deep 'The Bride to be!'
"Those were her words and one of ready wit,
"A bright and merry girl with nimble fingers, wrote
"What she did utter there, and much merriment
"The girls did have o'er me whom they were pleased to style
"Madam Abolitionist, a name quite odious
"In view of fact that some, my mates, there liv'd in land of slaves
"Which made me think they looked at times askance upon me.
"Ne'erless the words I copied and oft the lines pored o'er,
"And brought them home for fond remembrance sake
"Ne'er thinking more of them until this hour here."
  Lincoln had listened intent, and in his surging mind
One passage of the lines did o'er all others strike
And render them as naught—she, "The Bride To Be."—
A meaning his deep nature now in its solicitude
Did seem to grasp—did but too surely gauge.
It mattered not, if she were ne'er his bride, but only "Bride To Be"—
A subtle diff'rence which he with clearness saw.
Subtle! How tame the word as fine distinction swelled
Huge as a mountain in his mind distraught!
Slight shade of meaning, as might to others seem,
Yet, distinct and clear its drear and dark import
To view of him, now hurled to depths of woe
Despite himself and recent cheer; for he was one
Who believed in the occult, not knowing why he believed
But schooled thro' boyhood days in things of wood and air,

With varied promptings fraught, on lone and dim frontier
With vaulted heavens o'er,—roof of that Temple great
From which he drew his lore,—imbibed the mystical
And dreamt strange dreams in shady wood and sunlit plain,
Weaving weird fancies oft on mound of lonesome glade
With naught his mind to jar, but one vast stillness round
As if Creation paused and whispered unto him.
  So, prone to sense things of the veiled and weird
Of mystic realm where first his lips had lisped
He gleaned his knowledge of the world of men
Thro' larger, keener vision which caught each ray of light
That flash'd his way thro' dim leaf-lattic'd wilds,
Taking its hues from all the fantasies
Of untamed Nature's realm; and he, apt student e'er,
Did con each lesson o'er and deeper sense discern
In ways and things, than wast to others given.  And, tho' mystical
And e'er impressed by meanings vague, there was no wish to delve
In world of the unreal whilst life about him held
The pressing need of hand and heart and e'er ascending cry
Of those who struggled o'er the rugged road
To mortal lot assigned.  And, so enough there was
Of belief in those faint voices that oft the spirit wake—
Deep, far notes of mystic self—to make responsive e'er
The tense-strung chords of being; and thus the Seeress' words
Did grate, and make him brood as one assured too well,          [have.
The bodings from occult source remote didst there truth's sanction
  And she, noting his lapse did gently lift her voice
To strains e'er sweet to him when she most earnest was:
  "I have lived," she said, with look ineffable,
"In sunshine of your love and kind attentiveness
"To such degree that all happiness long years could give
"Would not excel what I in these short months have known
"So, content am I to pass, though if it were my will
"I here with you would bide and hap'ly minister
"To your dear needs and e'er rejoice the while
"O'er such sweet privilege, and watch with glowing pride
"Your rise to fame and usefulness—your set destiny;
"And you, O love of mine! at peace must be
"Whene'er the hour comes, for it is not remote,
"For I, in dreams have heard celestial choirs sing

"Such strains as ne'er before ecstatic sense did greet,—
"Volum'd music glad,—such waves of melody
"As fill'd my soul with joy and raised from earthly things
"My being rapt, as one who from a lofty mountain views
"Wide land below and feels in that high realm
"Apart from things that clog and cling, and ne'er descent doth crave
"Since taste has had of what the higher brings,
"Transcending joys of past that e'en loftiest hope inspire."
    Thus said, she gazed at him with eyes of tenderness
As if averse to causing pain, yet thinking mayhap to ease
Impending stroke when it didst fall, him in mind alone
And ne'er herself, he sole in her solicitude.
    Yet, unreconcil'd he held his mood and shook a dreary head,
Then speaking low, in voice of hollow sound,
As if the words did come from pained and saddest depths:
    " 'Tis not in man to feel a thankfulness for that
"Which breaks and bruises and robs his life of joy,
"Reversing Nature's course—blasting where bliss would be,
"Turning meadows green into sour, barren soil,—
"Mocking affections true and thwarting holy love
"That sets its value high—e'en high as Heaven's dome
"Whence it proceeds,—since Love is Heaven-born—
"So why should suff'ring come thro' love that us uplifts
"And thus undoing, make love its own torment!
"Why should souls be rack'd and know an anguish keen
"Beyond what Conscience holds 'gainst him who does a crime,
"Making our lives an agony when cruelly deprived,
"As if at source divine, e'en as a two-edge sword,
" 'Twas made for joy or pain, howe'er the whim might be!—
"Of life or Death the instrument, a Thing of bliss or woe
"Which may to Heaven raise or to Purgatory plunge;
"And I, victim of worst,—I thus am singled out,
"I, who love so much with flame so strong and pure—
"Must know Love's cruel self and drink from bitter cup
"As if offense it were to feel the being soar
"And gain some joy on earth, since we must tarry here
"Midst human miseries, the denizens, for time,
"Tho' not by own volition come,—unjust to me as seems,
"Who ne'er harm'd other knowingly, but e'er reverse didst aim;
"So, if sacrifice must be to Love's sheer savagry

"Why I, the chosen one!  I whose treasure sole, is she
"Of whom they wouldst me rob and leave me broken and undone!
"Others have loved and wooed and known the joyousness,
"Thro' all the ages past, e'en to this, which darker seems
"Than those of blood and fire back in Night of things,
"Since black Night it means for me o'er all Earth's bound'ries wide,
"And Night is Night in world throughout to all who suffer so!"
   She raised her hand, with other press'd unto her breast
As if to still heart-throbs, and, in clear even voice
Bad'st him pause and think how fleeting all things were
Of earthly cast, and grieving soul resign,
E'en as didst others, thro' the ages gone,
Since all do come to same unvarying end,
And, in tones of moving sweetness said:
   "The Past is but a mausoleum wherein lies the dust
"Of endless worlds of beings, from Time's beginnings strewn,
"Each particle so sentient once, e'en there to atoms come
"To float impalpable on air and with the vapors mix
"In Earth's strange chemistry and still mayhap have use
"In ways we know not of, with naught of them survived
"To earthly sense of touch, or sight, or consciousness,
"Save of their deeds the fruits, and mem'ry,—
"Some more than others beauteous and bright,—
"As their set parts they play'd on this, the earthly plane
"Ere they stepp'd off, as those who bow their leave
"In fair withdrawal meet, from others' presence here,
"Leaving howe'er, as mystic vine, invisible yet strong,
"That which twines the heart around of those to them affined
"In tie of love, or friendship dear, sprung from the plant of Love
"Which lives when all else wanes and withers low,—
"Essential core of all, from Time's ravages immune,
"Enduring as the orb that gives to Earth its light
"And, e'en as it joy-laden, with power infinite
"O'er life and Destiny, the spring that moves us all.
   "So think of this, O love! when I shall hence have passed
"And, empowered am to be with you indeed,
"Filling your being all with spirit of myself
"Not e'en as now you know, but perfect then and pure,
"Mingling with soul of you, reinforcing e'er
"When heaviness doth press and make your pathway dim;

"Bringing light where darkness is, e'en as a housewife fair
"To husband lone who sits in broody chamber dense,—
"With touch of loving hand and music of kind voice,—
"So shall I be to you—e'en more than earthly tie,—
"Yea truly more, heart of thy heart, soul of thy soul for aye."
    He look'd at her, a far sadness in his eyes that showed
The load that lay within his breast, and held
His pale lips mute—one long and sorrowing look,
As quest'ning there what joy would be for him
In honor e'er to rise, e'en in distinction great,
With her no more;—a thought he scarce could brook,
And bowing head on hands his face did cover full,
Moved to the act by surge of inward grief,
At sight of which her gentle bosom heaved,
And she with pity deep for him, quite overcome,
Sobb'd audibly and drew him from himself,
And kneeling by the cot with outstretched arms he clasped
Her form to him in soothing silent pledge
Of that great love, to speak which words were weak,
And thus did hold until her grief had passed
And she, as a child wearied, on his shoulder slept.
And so, for space it was, when he her head did place
On snowy pillow, with troublous thought that himself mayhap o'ertaxed
Her store of strength,—that which was most her need,
And, ling'ring only to see 'twere helpful, natural rest,
Tipp'd softly from the room to find obliviousness,
If such for him could be, on long-deserted couch.

# BOOK II

## I

*Lincoln betakes himself to his room and retires to rest but his sleep is broken by distressing dreams, in one of which he sees his sweetheart dead and stands by her bier while mournful ones gather about him. Awaking with a feeling of horror, he rises and, having dressed, walks forth in the night, seeking to divest his heart of the load that lies upon it.*

Dreaming again he thought he saw her dead
And, that life for him was as a withered tree;
And there was quiet stir and touch, and garlands in her hair,
And the white hands like wax were on her bosom clasped,
And women came and went and softly moved about
With hush throughout the house as if the world stood still.
And sorrowing faces showed where'er his eyes did turn,—
Great bearded men drawn there from farm and shop and mill,
In whisp'ring converse standing, vast pity in their looks
As tho' t'were the Last Day and all strife on Earth had ceased.
    And, he thought,—in throes of aching strain and stress
Of his great woe,—his mind would not accept
Her death as real, but ever clung to belief,
All self-imposed, that she would wake and look and smile at him,
A belief, yet not a belief, since buoyed by baseless hopes
And Fancy's figments frail, at which he fiercely plucked,
As drowning man at fitful gleams will clutch
And all unstable things in last despairing strife
For life there forfeit. And, with breath indrawn stood he and watched
For sign so long'd,—faint move of waxen lids,
Or haply flutter there of long and out-turned lash,
Or slight suffusing flush o'er white of marble cheeks
That wouldst denote return to mortal consciousness.
    But vain the hope! And then he thought he grew
Reproachful of the One, the All Dispensing Will,
That held her lock'd in cold and drear embrace
And wouldst not, to her, so dutiful and loved,

73

The boon of life vouchsafe where such vast craving was,—
Such heart-hunger pangs and yearnings,—and then, to the Unseen
He thought he call'd to mind the miracles thro' Him,
The Son, and Savior of mankind, and pleaded piteously
That power again might there be manifest
And she restored, e'en as were they of old.
    Was not the child of Jairus from state of death upraised!—
She, who, with waxen face and snowy garments lay,
E'en as the dear one here, with her dark curling hair
In fair ringlets clustered round unruff'd forehead white!
Could grief be more o'er her than here o'er his beloved
To move the Christ to pity and bring the flush of life
Back to her cheeks,—she whose loss to him were as death-sting itself!
    And in his heart he hoped, not daring breathe a prayer,
From sense innate that Faith was lacking, yet contrarily
Chafing within o'er fact of hand Divine withheld,
And grieving 'gainst the thing that robb'd his life of joy,
And in his mind half forming wild design to snatch
The frame so lov'd and bear it far away
To lone and hidden place, to live and e'er attend her dead,
She, his bride, in sense that where her clay wouldst lie
That sacred spot her bridal-bower should be.
    Thus his brain in cunning wrought, and fleeting fancies had
Of way to o'ercome Death,—at least to draw its sting—
E'en thro' mind atrophied, and in the dream he thought
A fierce glad feeling seized him o'er the triumph sensed
O'er drear Destroyer, and made his heart exult
That his great love for her didst e'en baffle Terror-King himself.
    Then he awoke with start, amaz'd and horror-chilled
O'er what his slumber brought, and in a daze arose
And groping forth looked out on dim of summer night,
And, tho' darkness held, it suited well his mood,
So shaken he and shorn of wholesome cheer,
And dressing in heaviness, he stalk'd from chamber there
And sought the care-free air, all laden with the breath      [things,—
Of glad season's fragrance,—of plant and flower and varied scented
Of tufted grass, young leaf of tree, and tender, peeping growths
That teeming Earth sends forth, the balm of rarest blend,
To glad the heart and lift the spirit high.
    And o'er his head the stars like silver studding shone;

And low on horizon the clustered Pleiades,
Like bright white gems in mat of turquoise set,
Did tell that night still held and heavy hours lay
Before the saffron glow that heralds coming morn
And long'd relief from such soul-agony intense
As he there knew.  So down the silent road fared he
With all Creation still in this, his tragic hour,
And vast loneliness of plain, illimitable, as seemed,
As the wide sky above, he faint entity,
Upbearing burden great that ev'ry fibre strained
Until he fain would cry aloud to ease his misery.          [breaking,
    And as he walked each shrub and tree thro' faint morn-light there
Did seem as mournful yew that weeps o'er lonely graves,
And he fancied then—illusion strange!—he glimps'd her resting place,
As momentary flash from out the drape of years,
And then in voiceless pain he long'd for light of coming sun
That he might gaze upon her, she yet in flush of life
For, was it not a dream?  Yea! a dream but one that held
A prophecy of that which in near future lay.
    The thought did follow quick on other cheering one
But he, by will's exertion, thrust it from him sharp
And sternly bade it go, whilst fierce in eagerness
To ruling fact he clung that in the flesh she was,
And, in such consciousness, did feel his spirits soar
And in his heart did hear the words that music were—
    "She lives! she speaks! she has not passed away   ᐧ
"But waits to welcome me beside her couch again!
"She still can smile and flash her wit at me!"
    Thus he communed and in new consciousness
Hugg'd to his heart—as she who snatches life
Of her dear one from crushing wheels in wild delirious joy—
The form beloved, in fancy, by reaction swept
To glad reality, to one and sole essential truth ᐧ
Grandly predominant—she lived and was as last he saw
When leave did take but few short hours since.
    And on he walked, lighter of step, in access new of joy—
New strength of limb, of mind, of being—altered quite,
A lilt in gait and poise, as if a miracle had wrought.
The wondrous change and him lent wings where erst were leaden feet,—

Such potency hath Thought—and by roadside there, down in the dust
And sent his voice aloft in fervent thankfulness          [he knelt
That she was yet in life, his own to clasp and claim.
    Then rising, on he press'd in strange delirious joy,
Throwing strength in ev'ry step, moving in strident gait,
The stars and deep night sky close at his beck and nod,
So friendly they and he so potent, and those wide level wastes,
Where rude-wall'd homes of hardy settlers were
Seem'd as a garden that he might with ease o'er leap,—
So light now grown and e'en so strong,—to shift of feeling due.
For he had grappled with dark brood and won,
Driving it far hence, locking and barring door
Of inward Torture-House, and felt now a force within
That all resistless seemed,—such force as might e'en worlds o'ercome
And to his will all mankind sway—a power measureless,
Not of himself, but the mere nucleus, he,
As one who at throttle sits and by turn of hand
Doth send the mighty engine forth wide Continent to span;
O'er all of which like strain of rarest music rose
The sweet refrain: "She lives! 'twast but a dream!"

# II

*The heart-broken lover at length finds a measure of relief in his walk and appeal to reason. His future and that of the West, with which his lot is cast, in the scale.*

And on he strode, or soared, in his rapt being's lift,
Small town and haunts of men there all too scant of space
For sweep of thoughts that surged like o'ercharged stream
Upbearing him afar o'er plane of wonted self,—
Transition not unknown, but of unwonted grandeur here,
For he from Childhood-days had felt the throbs and thrills,
The quiv'ring strains of joy, and voiceless ecstacies
By Nature's marvels rous'd,—the glad of sun-set glow,—
The drift of fleecy clouds 'neath vaulted blue that float,—
And all the glories of new-awakened life
That budding spring-time knows when languorous balmy air
Doth waft sweet messages,—to heart and mind thrice welcome e'er.
   So 'neath the stars he walk'd whilst the wide world slept,
His Destiny deep hidden the mists of years behind,
Yet, hopes and longings, great as bounds of universe;
And soon, more sober mood prevailing, he did dwell on things
That link'd him with the past,—the deeds of mighty men
Who o'er great world of action strode and bore their part thereon,
Voicing vital thoughts and living doctrines high!
He there recalling such and wond'ring if e'er might be
A place of mark for him beyond the irksome plane
Of drudgery and drear repression,—by circumstance held down—
When all his being craved, as wretched Bondsman, chained,
The boon of larger life.  And then his thoughts did turn,
To those, whose lot was his, and there was that within
Which warmed and made him glad, for he their heart-throbs knew,—
He of nature large, by jostling worldly aims, unspoiled,—
To helpfulness e'er school'd,—to all self-int'rest stranger quite,
Himself e'er least in mind, but weal of those who toiled,
Bending o'er bale or sheaf, or plow in spacious furrowing field,
First in thought,—he helpful friend to all.
And as he walked and mus'd his mind did image there

77

The fruits of days to come, by hardy settlers won
When West should grow, e'en as hadst the older realm
Whilst other but late had lain as great unbroken wild;
And, with nap of newness of the East worn off,
She mellowing into sober age, would come,
As comes to bees o'ercrowded in the hive,
That which strikes and deeply stirs in breast of man,
Breeding unrest, and, in voice insistent e'er
New moorings prompting; and far o'er sunward way,—
In steadfast stream they flow, whilst before their eyes in view,
With outer finger crook'd, bright welcome on her face,
Stands ample West e'er beck'ning,—West, great open door
In Nation's Mansion vast, with gate wide-flung for all.
    And there apace the hardy pioneers,
With wives and little ones and goods of family-pact
Did throng the ways and press from Earth's four winds
Bringing in their train, not least of 'sorted things,
New hopes, new Zeal,—new modes of life and thought,
Ideas varied, fresh;—e'en as to great world-mart,
The countless vessels come from divers climes and flags
And make wide harbor gay o'er unreck'd riches brought
With plenteous tasks for all,—where brawny arms are swung
And busy figures glide,—on deck, on plank, on wharf
With share of wealth for those who do their part and strive.
    And as he mused there came on him a calm
Of soul and mind, the equipoise of those,
The two extremes, bounds of his joy and woe
'Twixt which he, oscillating, knew, and he saw wisely then
In things which erst perplexed, this, his master-mood
E'er bringing to his soul a sense of sureness strong,
Sequel to inner struggles as to inner wretchedness.

# III

*He reaches a Camp of Gypsies in a wood by the roadside, where the Queen, Zelda, recognizes him as one who had served her and her people a good turn when a churlish settler would have had them driven from the neighborhood. She reminds him of the favor and to please her he enters her tent to have the future made clear to him.*

Then, as his mood, serene now grown, from spirit-tossings won,
To pace more measured led, his eyes observant, caught
At object nigh beyond, where road and woodside met,—
A scene that hark'd in fancy back to weird Arabia's realm,—
The Land of Eld, of ways unchanged, in spice and incense rich,
A mystic clime and strange, apart from others set,—        [touched,—
Realm slumb'rous, shadowy, profound, ne'er by world-progress
Dream-like, unreal as 'neath Enchanter's spell,—
Land of legend-charm and past'ral customs old,
Yet mark'd by hoof and lance of wild Bedouin hordes
That pack-train Trader knows, as knows lone desert-trail,—
Such scenes by sight suggested;—a group of Nomads dark
On e'er unresting round, e'en as in Patriarch-day
When flocks and herds were all and godly men did rule,—
They who onward fare nor clime nor Country know
But free as air, for aye have Nature's bounty claimed
And ne'er her hints have ta'en that toil increaseth store,—
Time-honored secret shown that makes World's Nations great,
By them alone ignored as not the Gypsy part;
E'er shunning wall'd abodes, wide earth alone their home,
Its ample breast their bed, its herbage waste the fare
Of faithful creature-kind that stall nor manger know.
    There, motley group of tents with listless life astir
And tethered beasts in view and swarthy men, as well,        [bright—
Fierce of twirl'd mustache, in velveteen, and pond'rous gew-gaws
Gorgeous in braid and band and varicolor'd things
That head or neck adorn'd and lent them aspect gay—
To whom lone walker came and friendly greeting gave
And greeting like received, with new accession then

In one, a woman bronz'd of teak-wood color rich,
With dark eyes luminous,—a midnight darkness deep—
Unfathom'ble as space—hair and brow in hue the same—
And queenly in walk and pose—a Dame of conscious power
Whose look full piercing was, as that which straight would read
What breasts of others hid and all unerring see,
The secret springs behind,—and this, with her the least
Since eye unmatch'd didst read the universe,
Else why such calm repose, unruff'd by doubt or fear—
A look unflinching e'er, unwav'ring, the gaze of certitude
With ne'er sign of lapse nor break where doubt could lodgment find!
    For she, in pose and mien, was calm as stars above—
'Neath whose guard she seemed,—by worldly jars unmoved.
Hers, not the awe of Kings nor Thrones, nor Nations born to pass,
Nor things by men deem'd great that minds of others sway;
Steep'd in lore of the Occult all such to her were naught;
But born to belief in that at tribal fount instilled
She held her course e'er true, firm in her forebears' faith,—
They, bronz'd and ton'd as she by sun and winds of varied climes—
Anchor'd as she, child unawe'd of long descended line
To that strange life apart in which liv'd they and passed—
Why should she care when Empires groaned and toppled into dust
Or joy o'er State new-reared, since e'er to her the same!
Aloof from all world-passions she, what matters then the trend
Of Life's unquiet ones, in self-made bondage held—          [spoiled!
Creatures of Culture soft by sweets o'er-fed, by much o'erpetting
    Not hers such life—she far as space of planets moved
From all nerve-racking cares,—the penalty e'er paid
For boon of strain'd existence won,—she with her lot content
No int'rest other:—to her and hers no shining pomp of state
In brain of man conceived appealing, e'en if e'er thought is turned,
Tho' languidly, its worth t' appraise—they, the unleaven'd ones
Of Earth's assimil'd clay, who of man ne'er favor asks
Save to unmolested be to go their chosen ways
Unchanged, unchanging with no herding e'er
In walls by mortals reared, nor set restrictions, soft,
By Social cult laid down, time-honored guiding lines
That wouldst them from simple past'ral life allure.
    Such thoughts, or others like, might well his mind there fill,
As he, erect, in silence stood and homely camp surveyed,

Noting beasts in sleekness bright,—from head to fetlock clean,—
Till mov'd to turn, her look to meet and beck'ning finger see,
Impressive, grave, the face and form of her,
Lore of Mystic East in eyes and mien exprest—
A look all wise, as mightst life's deepest riddles read,
A full-compelling force that him drew in her wake
To Central tent hard by, in ante-room whereof
Did table show and stools—on either side, the last—
Inner on which sate she and motioned him to first.
    Then as they, settling, sat, elbows on table propped
She gaz'd in silence mark'd, with full, frank look at him,
With eyes not such as e'er his sight had rested on,—
Unfathom'd velvet depths, to wondrous softness lit,—
A lustre-light 'yond speech, of moving potency,
Deep 'yond search of mind, howe'er in wit acute—
Eyes that thro' his frame sent instant thrill intense,
As touch of magnet does, save temper'd there the shock,
And made to tingle thro' his kindl'd being, all,
Heart first to feel the pierce, alarm-bell of the house
That being's myst'ries holds,—a lightning flash of joy—
A shaft of ectasy, which brought swift thought of her,
His one heart's love, and more endeared her then,
Quick'ning his consciousness,—as if translated swift
To high new state and rapt, with latent powers roused
To strength immeasurable, and longing tense that she,
The treasure of his life, might be with him to share.
    Then, in eyes so steadfast bent, shining as mirror-lake,
He thought he somehow glimps'd in their unfathomed depths
The rays of a vast pity, and, with chill he clos'd the gate
'Gainst dreary troop that wouldst make free with him
And plunge him into gloom, with her their minister,
Resolving her to hear with mind 'gainst credence set
And thus the brood outwit that wouldst his hope destroy.
    Then she, as if divining all, did break the silence deep
With kindly courtesy that much to him appealed.
    "You honor me," she said, her head inclining low
And speaking in a voice like deep orchestral chant,
"In coming without parley, by civil prompting brought,
"Which shows your nature well, for no light thing my act

"In calling you to come, since I have much to say        [proffer her
"That Future great, affects.   No!—Keep the silver!" when he did
A well-worn piece; "for I and mine already paid, and well,
"By what you did for us when churlish one set out
"To have us driven hence and sought of you advice,
"How best he might proceed! well knowing you were wise
"And, himself, mistrusting, leaning on your strength
"And finding better guide in that contact with one
"Immeasurably above—as eagle is to hawk;—
"One who made clear to him what heartless thing he aimed,
"And, having turned his mind, did use the noble words,
"As basis of his creed, his guiding star of life,
" 'Live and Let Live'—the base likewise of Gypsy belief,
"And rule of being,—words which should in brightest gold be writ.
    "God's sun doth shine for all—on stately palm and wayside weed as
"E'en as permeates His spirit the universe throughout:        [well,
"And he who dwells 'yond break of the wide river's flow
"Is not a rogue because he bides on other shore from him
"Who looks beyond and sees before his eyes
"Dim bank and wood and fields, all strange and unexplored,
"When boat, or skiff or raft that would'st bring face to face
"Would show he human is and civilized as well,
"With due enlightenment of soul and heart and mind:
"And you, from lofty prompt, did there make clear to him,
"Who meditated ill, the wrong he set to do
"To those who harm'd him not and who no others wrong
"Despite the fancy tales that flit from ear to ear
"And stir the country up, all crude inventions, cheap,—
"Tales that rise from harsh uncharity, in main,
"With ignorance to aid and prejudice conjoined:—
"Qualities whereof the world has plenteous store
"And e'er will have until the light pervades
"The corners dark that in man's being lie,
"Which make him think that he who bears a crooked nose,
"Or lives 'yond river's flood, in place he knows not of,—
"Away from rocks and trees that e'er familiar are,—
"Objects that self doth centre insensibly around
"In life's routine o'er same hard narrow path—
"Are villains, e'er, to be warned against and watched:—
"Such ones as build hostility 'gainst those to them unknown,

"Who speak, mayhap, a language strange, and diff'rent customs have—
"All, all to be condemn'd by those in denseness thus,
"Including not unletter'd lowly ones alone
"But those who sables flaunt and in rich jewels shine
"Preening themselves o'er high enlightenment.
"Kindness doth show the heart, and mark gentility,
"Whilst lack of it reveals the one to strain of baseness born.
   "So that is said in outpour and enlargement too
"Of gratitude for lofty thought exprest—
" 'Live and Let Live,' that saved harassment much,
"Which must our lot have been had ignorance prevailed,—
"Broad charity in you which shows your nature great,
"One of few, revealing spark divine,
"That like the sun doth ray for all, lowly and high alike,
"For which, kind Sir, you have the Gypsy Zelda's thanks,
"And so of all the tribe and world-suff'rers, as well."
   Thus said, she looked at him again, a long and steadfast gaze,
Then nodding head did mutter as her eyes did fall—
" 'The same! the same! and onrush now will come!' "
   Then, addressing him direct in low and even tone:
"Let me your hand now have, for I do feel opprest
"O'er sight of those in throngs, that whilst I here discourse,
"Like children let from school do crowd your horoscope,—
"A clamor and upstir as if the world did break,—
"Portent sure of mighty Change in life of you enwrapt,—
"Such deaf'ning sounds my ear-drums ring and all do surely tell
"No common lot is here but one that rides the hills
"And draws the faith of men—of worlds! I might well say—
"In vital things that in you centre strong.
   "Ah, such the rising is, the wild acclaim, and din and uproar high,
"That scarce own voice I hear:—the tumult of the years
"That doors of Time have burst and in disorder rush
"To cast off heavy packs and show the wondrous stores
"Each to its goal hath brought;—a wild disordered throng—
"As those in waiting-mass, bid to some grand levee,
"Who patience lose and irksome barriers break
"And, pell mell rush, each for himself the aim,—
"So, throng events, swift-rising here, that all unduly press
"And order lose, with jar and jostle rude,—
"Phantom show of things in store,—of what now the Future holds

" 'Midst which those yet unborn shall have their stirring part;—
"A dreadful din, with beat of drums and clash of deadly steel
"And high terrific roar, the voice of monster guns,—
"The hurtling shot and shell!—the fearful cannon-scream!
"The mass'd advance and contact—the crash and groans and cries
"As men do fight and die,—brother's hand 'gainst brother turned!
"The shatter'd ranks and closing gaps 'midst swirling smoke and flame!
"The awful gage of war! Chaos and Night in strife with lusty Day!—
"The threads of sequence cut and all ebulliant and wild
"The jumble here displayed,—flouting Time and dueness fair
"With naught to show, of meaning faint, why all the hubbub is
"Save that with ye it hath concern in some connection strange,—
"Ye the Magnet sole that fiercest lightning draws
"And so its havoc shown in presence premature,
"E'en as voice of Prophets rose in days of Shepherd kings
"And pointed that to be which yet in future lay.
    "Yet—patience! the outlook clears,—the mists subsiding all,
"As rush of pupils duly check'd, doth end in chastened ones
"In some brief let from desk where free exuberance was,
"Who, to wonted place repair and proper tasks resume;—
"So, tumult ceasing here, all warring throngs effaced
"Leave roots of meaning bared: Too fast hath lusty country sped
"Without precautions wise—this Genius of late day
"Whose youthful Might astounds! Not yet young Giant knows
"The family here a-rearing,—their varied bents and aims,—
"Old Adam that persists and blends in earthly clay—
"But building high ideals, with mind preoccupied
"He sees not the traits strong-mark'd in his domestic group
"Which, slowly germing mean for him in years to come
"A world of woe,—sees not—tho' prophesied by those
"Whom men call wise—the Menace grim, tho' in his wakeful ears,
"If he wouldst heed, its raucous voice must ring;          [o'erawe,
"Nor yet doth note a growing caste that wouldst bear down and
"All 'yond its Section-line; nor doth observe in those
"Who mark the trend the steadfast, quest'ning look
"Direct in others' eyes—a look that holds no fear—
"But boldly says they like not assumptions overmuch
"And may some time have cause their sense to make more clear,
"And if 'tis purposed Chinese wall to build
"Round those with Caste imbued within exclusive zone,

"Hands will be found its mass to fitly raze;—
"Divergence here revealed that vasty meaning holds,
"Fated in lapse of Time a fearful crop to bear,
"E'en as Pandora's box with all its brood of ills.
 "Yet, quite natural all, if we but pause and think!
"Of diff'rent mothers these,—traditions varying all,
"As climes and Creeds whence sprung;—dissimilar in race,
"E'en as in modes and manners,—life from unlike angles seen,
"As unlike standards hold,—unlike, since massive early weld
"When hammer-strokes of founders bold them into Nations forged,
"Each group in native ways ingrained, clogg'd with heredity,
"That conduct rules and veers to clannishness,—
"Old clutch of forbears holding, save in larger sense
"Where Freedom's emblem shines when bowed and bared behold
"All rev'rent, worshipful, o'er attribute divine
"Which, felt and understood, doth universal homage bring;
"From early serfdom thus reacting, as seemeth Nature's law,—
"Germania flaxen-haired, and staid Britannia's sons;—
"The hardy Scot and they of rugged Wales, heartsome, musical;
"And those of Erin's Isle, and they of Scandinavia's coast,—
"With dark-haired Gaul, and olive-hued of Tuscany—
"All here transplanted, as the wind-blown seed,
"Or that by ocean-current sent to find a lodgment sure
"On some far strand and there take root and grow
"Until its shoots o'er spacious land do spread,
"Finding welcome there in soil and climate meet.
 "E'en so regard bright New-World plant in crude incipience
"And say if busy Guardians, who have brought it so to bloom,
"Have not had load upon them, and of task aquitted well,
"Bringing seedlings thus, from varied climates blown,
"Unto fruitage rich howe'er may flavor varied be,
"And, commingling, giving and taking, each, unto the very brink
"Of vast abyss, which they must span or sink lamentably,
"Since from cause far-sprung old humours latent here must break
"To plague a goodly land, e'en as in past they plagued
"In ancient realms ere wast the New-World dawn;
"And so shall vex until doth rise from some dim source unseen
"The leader wise, the helm to seize and guide the troubled ship
"To waters fair and those mutinous put down,—
"A Captain fit, who, by tumult and uproar of greeting late,

"Must here in making be for coming stressful hour.
    "So they, from German forests drawn and storied Norseman's fiords,
"And they, of Britain's race, and likewise those
"In veins of whom is blood that humbled Rome,
"Must have their warrings, e'en though at Freedom's shrine
"After blest lapse, since they their hands in mutual faith and leal
"Didst join in pledge and great Sanctuary rear
"To hail and shelter those, by ermined Autocrats oppressed,
"And share thenceforth of the sweet edifice.
    "And clearly now I see the very root of all,—
"The baneful thing entwin'd that e'er contention breeds
" 'Twixt headstrong groups,—an ill that parent-sanction has,—
"Yielded in busy past of duties manifold,—
"Ere land had so progressed and finer sense did gain
"Of what wast other's dues and better conscience win,—
"When untried and young his lusty fledglings were
"With ev'ry heart in unity and no raven-note to mar
"The concord blest, to early years and strenuous, known.
    "A shift of scene!  Before my eyes, as Panorama vast
"The land all peaceful lies, where busy workers are
"At many tasks diverse,—in sense by climate ruled—
"Two grand Divisions there by artful Thermos drawn:
"The Sultry zone distinct, where torrid rays command—
"From other sections cleft, with Institution strange
"By others all unshar'd—a graft on New-World tree,
"From alien branch clipt off where beast thro' Jungle roams,
"With germ of native blight with it transplanted here!—
"A thing that gives unrest, destined in time to spread
"And bring turmoil and strife throughout the land itself.
    "That, for the future!  What now my eyes in rounding view behold
"Are busy heads and hands o'er all the land at peace
"With mark'd distinctions tho', as climes diff'rentiate:—
"The field of Humid zone, for rice and cotton famed,
"Alive with turbaned heads low-bow'd, 'neath the torrid rays,
"With badge of Helot-toil,—of enforced servitude—
"A thing surviving here, deemed ill in Joseph's day,—
"And subject since to untold thousands homilies;—
"When Egypt's Pharaohs reigned and held beneath their sway    [tilled.
"The myriad bondsmen drear that hewed and drew, and unrequited
    "Two other Sections large, from Sultry realm apart,

"One old, one new on Nation's chart with vast wild wastes uncleared,
"The elder first in view,—no face of blacks nor show of bondage there
"But different all,—from Slavery's blight exempt
"Thro' clearance made in not far distant past
"When baneful thing in harsher soil displayed but shallow root.
  "Two regions then distinct in Family-holdings show;
"No turbaned heads low bowed nor seas of cotton there,
"Nor fields of rice, nor stretch of cane-brake green,
"But thick, in elder realm the busy spindles hum,
"The smoke ascends, and steam,—a busy land of looms,
"Of mines and forge and mill—a zone of artisans,
"Of merchants, traders, shrewd, and varied Craftsmen skilled,—
"Centre and mart of Commerce—of Industry intense,—        [askance
"E'er viewed by realm of Planter soft, with arching brows and eyes
"As place of barter—from things genteel apart.
  "Of other realm that shows,—the forward, pushing pioneer
"In hardy task of ope'ing up for his and those unborn
"The vast unmeasured lands that lie where far declining sun
"Doth slant his rays, their soil to glad and cheer;—
"Those reaches vast of plains where untam'd Savage roams—
"Sections apart, these two, yet in aim and thought the same
"Since from Vulcan's realm pours sturdy offspring true,
"The tide to swell that o'er new land there sweeps
"Where glad free toil with willing hands and hearts
"In season due shall transform wilderness,
"E'en as their forebears did on that dim early coast,
"And launch new world with less of trials and toil.
  "Two sections thus defined,—from Sultry one apart,
"Save in sense of Family tie, e'en now by latter viewed
"With coldness ever growing, and, in keen return made feel
"Herself esteem'd nigh alien, since in thought, in trend and ways
"Shows diff'rence mark'd,—as one that o'er cow'ring creatures stand
"As overlord, and thereby lordly habits gain
"Which breedeth Caste, foreign to New-World soul and soil
"That sword of Freedom won from overlord o'er seas,
Hence ne'er reborn to be on land acquired so,—
"A lapse not unobserved by other twain that full accordant are,
"Who from same standpoint view and with equal fervor spurn
"The Institution dark, by other so upheld.
  "Now shifts the scene!  New omens plain in view disclosed,

"By uncleared section shown, whilst other fades away,
"And filling here wide space doth to the foreground press,
"In yellow sunlight bathed, its nearer outward fringe
"Teeming with peoples new, ardent, hopeful all,
"With Future great entrust, in those rich spacious fields,
"By willing toil made bloom, with ever watchful eye
"Toward Sultry realm that Bondsman's labor knows,         [there.
"And look that means the Thing contemn'd shall have no welcome
    "Yet—hold! the picture fades, and now in view appears
"The dom'd and marble pile, the stately storied Seat
"Of Nation's Council high wherein to all is shown
"Long years of wordy war,—the New World's growing pains
"Now in throes to be,—ne'er-ending turbulence—
"Rancor,—insult and bitterness—sharp retort and kindred thrust;—
"Acrimony e'er—recriminations,—challenge—collisions—discord
                    ceaselessly,
"Wherein great minds do grapple,—Titan 'gainst Titan hurled,—
"And where great names do flare and there make luminous
"The noted fray, and mark thro' Time an epoch quite unique
"In Nation's life, and then decline and pass and leave
"To others, burden drear of Sections' deadly feud;—
"Two Sections there 'gainst other, e'er seen thro' all, arrayed,
"Shoulder to shoulder brace'd, as still the voices rise,
"Oft sacrificing Truth for dazzling substitute,
"And all but blood-shed comes, when,—Lo! sleek Compromise
"Doth intervene, and artful way propose
"Whereby shall Bondage ne'er beyond fixt limits pass,
"At which they grasp, as men bent and wearied clutch
"At saving prop that serves to topp'ling building hold,
"In lieu of shoulders strained, that soon can hold no more,
"And so for time the troublous question sleeps.
    "It sleeps,—not healthful sleep, for, where is canker-growth
"What sleep can be, save fitful fev'rish rest,
"Disquiet in the blood that yields no peaceful hour,
"Drear consciousness of blight that e'er doth lie in wait
"And holds its victim tense in mortal dread and fear?—
"Such sleep is that,—a sedatated spell,
"By Nation's Solons wrought as from sick couch they fade,
"Good, well-meaning men, o'er self-approval light
"And gleaning comfort full as peaceful pillows press.

"What now is shown in golden haze emplaced,
"Where rounding country is, the interposing reign
"Of calm and quiet, normal days serene,
"Old wounds all healed and seeming unity
"The land throughout.  But here the veil doth lift
"And Sultry realm of Rice and Cotton, shows.
"Her wharves are throng'd, her docks with vessels packed
"And white-garb'd Planters pass and come, by sable workers hemmed,
"As barrel and bale are brought and swift aboard are rolled,—
"A busy scene and strange, as if the Indias swept
"Their wat'ry bound'ries o'er and sultry land had joined.

      "Alack! drear meaning comes as clouds o'er country rise!
"Not longer now shall realm of Planter rest
"Content with compact won o'er top'ling Passion's heat.
"Behold him rise and stir and don his jacket, brisk,
"And grasp lithe cane with fierce aggressive clutch,
"With eyes covetous turned toward fertile Western plains
"Where Ceres her bounty showers o'er loamy soil unfed,
"With stern resolve there form'd to beat the Barrier down;
"Same Council that didst make shall see the thing undone
"With all dispatch and wit whilst there his power holds,—
"A power saved if dark intent succeeds,
"A power lost if sicklied o'er delay;
"For, stripling West doth e'er in influence grow,
"A Lusty one—by all as Marvel hailed,—
"Young Hercules new-come 'mongst New World's Sections great.

      "Hence, sees the Sultry realm, with unmarr'd vision clear
"Full shorn her strength must be, the strength that dominates,
"If rests quiescent she and former Bargain holds—
"Delilah there to her, by blandishment undone;—
"She who the reins hath held and taken e'er high lead!—
"Place to be yielded ne'er whilst Family-pact endures.

      "What now doth loom is dark,—storm-clouds rolling low;
"From ev'ry side sweep they o'er land here all aroused        [drear,
"By drastic Act,—'gainst protests, threats and solemn warnings,
"In Nation's conclave voic'd—that saving Law repeals,
"Hurling guard-rail down for Slav'ry's march unchecked
"Thro' wide New West, all toils and stress despite,
"And pains and watchful care accursed Thing to stay,
"Exposing Virgin land to what its sons abhor."

She paused and raised her head, with eyes unseeing, save
What inward glimps'd and seem'd to meditate
Until again she bent with lids half-closed, cast down,
And forth resumed:  "What now I see and hear
"Denote uprisings vast o'er all the Section wide
"Where light of furnace flares and wheels of commerce hum,
"Where Oratory, transparencies and vivid Pageantries—
"Processions long, with lanterns, flags and waving banners bright,
"Do rule the hour and hectic make the face of land throughout;
"The Countryside remote, and distant vale and glen,
"Their bustling ones all pouring, the larger throngs to join,
"As rills and streamlets burst from tangled glade and hill
"And bounding forth the wider streams to greet
"And burden there unload, with all in turn to merge
"With creeks, and they again with rolling rivers broad,—
"So, outpour here of varied living floods
"That form the main, which now, by oratory lashed,—
"By tongue of leaders, large and small,—appeals of flaring prints,
"And all that rouse and stir the slow inactive blood          [beneath,
"To quicken'd purpose great—to swirl and eddy, Passion's foam
"And show a land upstirred as ne'er before was known
"Since that great day when alien bonds were burst
"And Tyrant rule o'erthrown in name of Liberty.
     "And now, o'er din and tumult,—vast confusion wild,—
"New voice doth peal, from wide Prairie raised,
"All-piercing, strong, ascending high and shrill,
"Like clarion-cry from roofless forum borne
" 'Neath limpid blue that Western clime beams o'er,—
"A voice that holds, in tense soul-searching thrill,
"E'en as the pibroch weird in far, vibrating strain,
"The clans that call'd from depths of glen and peak
"In Scotia's stressful day, their Chieftain's trials to share;—
"O'er Nation ringing loud and thrilling Patriot-ear,
"With trenchant words that monstrous doctrine scores,
"Baring preachments false, exposing Sophistry
"With logic merciless that shatters structure false
"Which wouldst young Statehood nip unless in compact fast
"With Slaveland's lords there joined howe'er much she loathed.
     "So ring those stirring tones, the air vibrating through
"O'er land of Freemen wide where people pause to hear

"And gleam of meaning catch, then in haste repair
"To house and hall, and leafy grove as well
"Impassion'd words to greet of those whose sense have caught
"Import of warning call to all who cherish dear
"The mighty Chart from belfry'd Hall proclaimed
"In Glory's Day, to rise and by might of Franchise high
"Unite and speed with force resistless, all,
"And save from shoals and rocks, 'neath Slaveland's plottings hid,
"The threatened wreck of State's great tossing ship.
    "Again a shift, and now wide level plain
"Bounded by horizon alone, as seems, vast in brilliant sheen
"Of rank, green-bladed growth, thick, luxuriant, rich,—
"Where Kansan freeman tills, with here and there displayed
"The horrid stain of blood that marks a settler slain
"In dire conflict of arms with base marauding hordes
"From fell Missourian shore,—hireling ruffian bands,
"To pester Kansas sent, and by Fraud and Force o'ercome
"Set aim of young free land, in lawful way, to bar
"Thro' time for aye, reproach of Slav'ry's blight;—
"A dreary strife that thro' the years shall run—
"Civil War, with horrors like, to Kansan-soil confined
"With will inert of him whose nerveless fingers hold
"Great Helm of State 'neath whited Dome afar,
"By lords of Bondsmen's realm his ev'ry action ruled,
"They, whose hands to place may lift and with same ease pluck down.
    "So thro' the years must Kansas bleed, her plea for Statehood
        stilled
"Unless yield she, as one full cowed, to Slaveland-master's voice
"And come fast-chain'd to blood-stained Jaggernaut,
"E'en more remorseless now since looms prize of West so large,—
"A proffer she, with bleeding breast and high disdain, e'er spurns."

# IV

*Having foretold the coming of the Civil War the Gypsy proceeds to relate the various expedients resorted to in Congress to placate the discordant elements, and ward off the strife which all see is seemingly inevitable. Lincoln's election to the Presidency foretold and the notable incidents that lead to the formation of the Party that elevates him to the high office.*

Then she, from trance-like spell emerg'd and ceas'd her far-ton'd chant
For moment there, and, upright sitting gazed,
Full on him,—he, attentive held and carried wonted self beyond,—
And noted int'rest deep the words in him had roused
And nodded wittingly as if in affirmation glad
O'er inward query which had doubt unquiet waked,
Now by his look allayed, and drooping her head again
Unfoldment strange in cadence low resumed.
"Once more a change! the land throughout in view
"With twain Sections great that in full accord are—
"In geography apart—in heart and mind as one—
"Aflame with smoking torch, and tissue lanterns gay,
"Transparency and flag, by eager marchers borne,
"Processions night by night and oratory high,
"From flag-deck'd platforms rais'd, 'midst close-mass'd hearers, tense,
"Their straining eyes and ears by ruling Topic held
"Discuss'd in ev'ry phase, with interest enhanced.
" 'Mongst young and old alike sweeps new contagion wide
"In swirling town, in hamlet small and wayside home as well
"Where'er men are, the Touch-tap light that sets the words aglow,
"Or bellows-sparks that flick portent of flame,
"In which loom Kansan's wrongs e'er large, vital to Freeman all,—
"His rights o'erborne at brazen bold behest
"Of Slaveland's lordly ones, on Ship of State supreme,
"Whose acts reviewed, made clear, with vividness portrayed,—
"Denounc'd 'midst wild acclaim, upflinging hats and cheers
"Throughout those Sections knit, by Helot-menace roused,—
"All showing time eventful come when choice of Ruler falls
"With Parties eager now to edge nigh Peoples' ears

"And pour the grains and chaff in which their wont to deal,
"With view to Suffrage great behind it all that lies.
  "And he, ta'en by those leal from far unbounded wastes
"Of New World's reach, on wide Prairie reared,
"In land remote, as they,—the chosen ones of old,—
"Appointed time to bide, their mighty work to do—
"How may I the fame here speak that sudden-risen shows
"And kindles spirit-like in souls of millions thrilled
"By magic of his name!—he, hailed through universe—
"Welcom'd by ev'ry heart, e'en as lov'd household prop,
"From distant journey back who on fond threshold meets
"The greeting warm e'en as the hearthstone glow.
"That speaks its welcome too, by wife and little ones endowed!—
"How may I speak when here in diffidence
"Sits he, and mildly tolerant, lets great Revealment pass
"As rustle of the leaf, or whirring sound of bird
"Or other things as trite, tho' that before me shown
"Is truth as fixt as stars, that night by night we see,
"As readily to fail as stars themselves to fall."
  A pause again, with head half-raised, partial inquiring lift,
Deep eyes upon him fixt, as if new int'rest waked
Thro' these enlargements shown, not e'en by her foreseen,—
Long earnest gaze, as, seeing matured and so in vital play
The powers thus forecast, as likewise events of mark
Which future held,—things immature, or formless,—inchoate,—
All, all, the actual there, forceful reality,—
Late Present thrust in Past, the span of years annulled,
And he, with such great Heritage before World's eyes in truth!
And so she curious look'd, as she wouldst compass there
Secret of change so great that Time's due lapse must bring,—
Such transformation vast when he, Earth's cynosure,
Wouldst shining loom,—Posterity's as well;
And satisfied at length her head she bent again
And pressing hand to brow continued as before:
  "When Changes great impend in Nations as in men,
"Things casual or slight assume celerity in growth,
"Or so to sense appear, as if by latent power spurred:
"The sun in Western sky, as golden orb is poised
"On edge of wide-world rim, doth seem no more to move
"With stately pace, but sharply speed accelerates

"And slips from sight as if with wish to pass
"And have the plunge quick o'er, suspense there unprolonged,
'As in his wake close-press'd comes swift diurnal Change,
"The dark-robed Night that all wide land enshrouds,
"As knowing well her rights, and taking place supreme
"In 'pointed course,—her reign distinct and diff'rent quite.
    "And when, in lives of Nations, faring on apace,
"Sunsets of eras come the parting guest is sped
"Leaving house to clear and brisk new order know,
"And in stir and haste, excitement that e'er marks
"The break from former ways, the small have potency
"And what doth tiny seem may hence a mountain loom,
"Grains of things affined that coalescing, form
"The rock that rives a State, or sends a Throne headlong;
"And if to Nations so why not to parties, too?—
"Organs of Power mere, that have their rise and wane
"At choice of Freemen's will, the Arbiter-in-Chief
"Who suffers much to pass e'er stern Assertion comes,
"Mayhap from breath of words from Spokesman high in trust
"Of ruling Conclave proud, at psychic juncture voiced,
"Which brings a storm that tears the seasoned stanchions down
"Of stately Ship of Rule, sweeping as feather light from jealous-guard-
"The luckless one that steered despite the lashings strong,    [ed helm
"Leaving naught but wreck for other hands to clear.                    .
    "So now, 'midst blast and blare is wondrous canvass on,
"Men's deep convictions stirr'd, all things high magnified
"In keep with spirit tense that unblurr'd vision knows,
"And unclogg'd will as well, the mind divest of pack
"Of worldly petty things and left in pristine strength—
"From self-piled burdens freed—by call of Need released—
"E'en as cry ascending now, the Patriot-heart to thrill,
"With Nation all upwrought,—the Ruler-makers roused,
"And speeding to and fro on varied tasks and quests,
"Commingling dense in street, in hall and rural grove,—
"Primal place of meet of ancient ones,—effaced,—
"In misty day when man more rude and rugged was,—
"They great and small by self-same ardor warmed,
"Toilers where'er—at grimy bench, or blast or board
"In forge or mill, or yet 'mongst singing spindles brisk,—
"To new importance thrust with Day of Suffrage nigh,—

"Of mighty Franchise-Right which in such time at least
"Doth make proud spirits meek,—doth see smug Seekers bend,
"With care solicitous o'er ev'ry ill that lies
"In human Family's path, as if no peace would know
"Till all were lifted high where ease and plenty are.
    "And now, 'yond bounds of Sultry Realm behold!
"Damon and Pythias-like, those two link'd Sections, leal,
"Each high in warm resolve, each jubilant o'er hopes,—
"Young hopes new-born—new issues, isms, all
"With him, whose clarion call has things to focus brought,—
"High choice of those who life and vim on Party new bestow—
"For lofty Seat by People's voice acclaimed,—
"He who hears my words as hears he sighing winds
"So modest he—incredulous as well—
"Yet Truth ne'erless, for, what is to be will be
"And Zelda naught doth read save that which comes to pass!—
"He, magnet there that Patriot-mind attracts
"Palladium high to country's hope and weal.
    "Yet what has hap'd to make young David bold?
"Why that high look and bearing unafraid?
"Has not Goliath stalk'd with ruthless tread o'er all
"Insulted, flouted,—Reason's voice e'er mock'd and laugh'd to scorn!
"With rasping tongue—derisive, sharp, belittling e'er,—
"Transforming Might to Right—heaping ill on ill,
"Viewing with rancor set, all those who dar'd dispute
"The whys and wheres of e'er o'erbearing will,
"With raucous laugh when high offensiveness
"Didst from abused e'en protest mild extort;—
"He ready e'er on Nation's floor in stately Council-Hall
"Sharp quarrel to pick and deal the bludgeon-blow
" 'Gainst those who differ'd;—Apostle loud of Separatist's creed,
"Holding nigh as aliens all averse in belief
"To sway of Caste,—he who e'er didst arrogate
"Sole right the Ruler's hands to guide,
"A task too easy late with those the reins that hold
"They yielding nerveless clutch to that imperious grasp
"With ne'er a word of warning when Coach of State careened
"Howe'er near in reckless drive dread precipice might be.
    "Then why, in Party upstir here, by Freemen's process caused,
"Due exercise of theirs the Ruler high to choose,

"Such confidence in hearts of young aspirants shown?—
"They, new-come on fateful field to test the unflesh'd blade
" 'Gainst steel of cohorts tried, in holds of Patron's favor trenched
"Invincible their bastion'd might, so seeming, that has erst defied
"Same young presumptuous ones, as others, and liv'd to laugh to scorn
"Attempts so futile all, to meet resistless power,
"Season'd and disciplin'd in artful crafty ways,
"For, e'er it fares as clan unbroke, by baleful Institution held,
"To matter else no heed that Country's weal may claim,
"Object alone in view that shall to Realm of Caste inhere
"With care e'er less for bond that States in Union hold,
"But meaning plain express'd that Sultry land doth shine
"All self-sufficient, with need of helpful ancient tie no more,
"And mooting the time to come when line of cleavage yields          [list,
"And Southern clime and Kansan plains, and, where else may Slaveland
"United course shall take and early pledge abjure
"And Nation new so build with Caste the reins in hand.

    "And thus on Country's hustings wide, united front e'er shows
"The Section petulant, with those accessions won
"Beyond its bounds the wide land o'er, by sop of office lured
"And artful preachment e'er to forebears' faith uphold,
"Fetish of Partis'nry—the dreary Shibboleth
"That e'er unreasoning clings,—grist to false Leader's mill.
"That wouldst sustain, howe'er in worth and virtue object fails.

    "Thus, late in past hath beamed on Party Arrogant          [day
"The face of Fortune glad,—Success foreseen,—and scarce eventful
"Of choice of Ruler comes, as now before so shown,
"That ripple anxious knew pending determ'ning hour
"That didst in summing prove discounted triumph won,—
"Such certainty there was o'er boasted end to be.

    "Yet not in vision now the outlook roseate!
"Wide change hath come,—their sun of years hath set
" 'Yond horizon of Night, and with another dawn
"New prospect there will be and a new-ordered house,
"With recent guest a mem'ry, save for warnings grim
"Such as the Parthian sends, with outcome soon to be
" 'Yond what the Parthian knew, and to all mankind show
"That Liberty, to hold, a strength must have within,—
"Not semblance mere,—and prove itself when called
"By worth its own, from seed Divine that springs."

# V

*The confusion in the Councils of the Party of the Slaveholder described, with the especial reference to the breach in the organization between the members of the North and those of the South.*

Then, with heavy sigh indrawn as if what yet she saw
All more o'erpow'ring was, again she rais'd her head
As a skilled diver does, upshooting from the deep
For breath of air above, where creature, man, belongs,
And gazing on his face saw ev'ry feature set
In tense absorb'd spell as if the years to come
Disburden'd were in truth, and he, there viewing all,
With mind still keen for more, insatiate, as seemed,
With inward urge to her, which she failed not to read,
And drooping eyes once more with chin upon her breast,
Proceeded as before to show futurity:
"When massive tree succumbs that storms of Time hath braved
"And in forest prostrate lies, as fallen monarch low
"The curious mind doth search to cause of ruin fix,
"Perplext that what seem'd strong should fatal weakness prove
"Till wise inspection there doth heart's unsoundness show,
"With all made clear, and then the wonder comes
"That life was so prolong'd; and thus 'mongst men it is.
"How strong soe'er they seem, howe'er combin'd they be
"In bond of mutual aims,—whate'er the favor high,
"In which they bask, if vital weakness is,
"Proud strength will fail in due and fateful hour.
    "And since Change so great impends, the break and overturn
"Of that which long hath held, the Thing of men accurst,
"And with it sundry ills, ungodly vicious brood,
"Of first and ranker, outgrowth these, the fruits of Sectionry
"At Nation's helm that sate as Party dominant
"Especial Cult to serve with influence e'er malign
"On sturdy race as whole,—oppressive, irritant,—
"Land's progress fair to clog and due expansion bar,
"Worth while it is in steady poise to hold,—
"E'en as pointed lens the shining worlds that scans

"And course of planets marks for signs and omens sensed,—
"The mind that chafes and strains and, with vision unobscured,
"Regard the current-swirls that to great centre tend,—
"The myriad rivulets by side accessions fed,
"To larger streams that sweep, as they to swollen floods,
"Tracing from local haunts of hill-side, vale, and plain,
"And mountain-slope and crest, Northland and Eastland o'er,
"And Western levels wide, and Lake-realm, forest-clad,
"The springs and sluices dense that babbling outflow pour,
"To hence and yon converge and country wide o'erspread,
"With gathered force intense, still forces more to wake
"That tax doth heavier bring 'gainst what but slightly holds,
"Anon with snap of strand and warning grim of stress
"That limit soon must reach of tense expanded strain
"And know abysmal break and vast epochal change.
    "So marks Transition-stage to Culmination's pitch,
"With all the land o'erswoln, the icy Zone aroused,—
"She, e'er slow to wrath!—and wide Prairie reach,
"With land of Caste upstirr'd,—hurried couns'llings oft,—
"Faces white and set, with lines of care seamed deep—
"Hats back from foreheads tipp'd as if the furnace-heat
"Where forg'd the thunderbolts, wast raised unwontedly,
"Leaving Throwers vext with minds in wild turmoil,
"All on part of those the Nation's Ship that ruled
"And there had carried high and lash of power snapt
"Demurring heads sharp o'er, cowing, enforcing e'er,—
" 'Till bluntly brought to book,—abrupt, prodigious change
"Thro' country's uprise great when rose the Tocsin-call
"From one ordain'd to lead and so New Order bring—
"Harvest of crop benign from hardy chosen seed
"Broadcast thro' hand full wise of Husbandman of skill
"And vision consummate of goodly yield to be.
    "The seed so spread, in Truth's alembic fine
"To breath of words resolves, wing'd words of Destiny
"With sequence fraught 'yond belief,—o'erwhelming, momentous!—
"Words fram'd to Query form,—with care adroitly timed
"Fateful as weapon e'er by hand of Master wrought,
"Tho' shap'd for Forum's launch and not for lurid field,
"Which ne'er effect couldst match howe'er might cannon roar,
"Or massive columns melt before onslaught of note;—

"Fateful Ithurial spear with mystic power charged
"The Sophist's garb to rend and crowning evil bare
"That Nation's strength had sapp'd and ceaseless discord bred,
"With risings, protests, clashes, oft, in Land of Liberty,—
"By lips of men so hailed, yet e'er with poison-drop
"In cup by people quaffed, with threat of poison more
"On part of pamper'd ones, in fam'ly group much spoiled,
"By o'er indulgence so and those deferrings soft
"And tendance obsequious, with honied flatteries
"That Slave to Master yields, enlarging vanity,
"Instilling small conceits which with their subject grow;—
"Distorting sense of rights to view irrational;
"Engend'ring false esteem and self-sufficiency;
"Giving bent, as natural so, to lord and domineer,—
"As children e'er uncurb'd who ne'er to others yield
"But wilful way must have howe'er to mates unfair;—
"As Class upgrown, abnormal,—exacting, and imperious,—
"To Caste exclusive hard'ning,—a land-Autocracy
"Superimposed on what 'neath its feet doth lie,—
"Black servitude itself, with naught of wholesome props nor stays
"Wide intermed'ate gap to fill, nor deem'd desirable
"By dawning Cult Anomalous, of sway supreme to be
"If fruits of plannings thrive and Hope's large measure fill,
"With spacious West the lure, the sum of strivings, all.
    "Thus alien they to native thought and aims,
"Toward Feudal day of eld reacting, with Bondage pilot-ship,
"With sails all hoist and set, belling imperious way,
"With steady trend and sure on Retrogression's sea
"To long abandoned coast of that uncivil realm
"Erst by lord and baron held, from hands of others wrest
"With Castled-keep and moat and drawbridge sinister
"And watch and warder rude, to all approach averse
"Yet, of rights of those 'yond pale not o'er particular,
"Living to full the sense, from hearts still unexpunged,
"That in exercise of sway, greater or less, in fine
" 'Tis not by scales of her, the Goddess blind, such rule,
"But, high avowed, uncouth, by churlish god of Might.
    "So theirs, of state that was, till in Time's balance weighed
"When walls didst crumble low and moated-waters fail,
"With creeping slimy pests usurping place of those

"Who in their day there lived and boist'rous ways pursued
"With passions unrestrained, e'en as the beasts of chase,
"And pomp of Prestige loud that ne'er gav'st Order let
"Impetuous blood to curb by Regulation just;
"And so wast Europe held for night of years in throes
"Till that which galled didst 'gainst itself react
"In confines stifling grown, and lives so liberate;
"For, e'er as shows the life intense there narr'wing process is:
"The stream swift-sent doth not in broadness spread
"But deeply ploughs and scores in madd'ning rush headlong,
"Of thirsty soils regardless,—its pressur'd walls between
"Precluding outflow wide and hast'ning inward sweep;
"E'en as so to men, hedg'd by own conceits,
"For rifts the mind may have, by vain desires digged
"And him the ground that yields, wholly in turn possess,
"By habit thus enslaved, Pariah to grace of impulse kind,
"No more mild Reason's voice to know, nor sweet amenities
"That smooth with gracious touch mankind's asperities,
"But ruled by Selfishness, next kin to Cruelty,
"Whence springs Reaction drear, world's wholesome pace to check
"And Wrongs and ills such breed as Time benighted knew,
"Lapse scarce perceptible since slow and faint the change,
"As castles in air that were, ere reared in massy piles,
"E'en as those of Past that served their rugged day;
"And hands their walls that raised have left successors skilled
"Such works to reproduce when falls the hour ripe,—
"The moody towers high,—portcullis, moat and trappings all,—
"Accompan'ments of Turbulence that recrudesence threats,
"A thing outleaven'd long that seemeth, the lapse despite,
"Its head anew to raise in place expected least
"If signs a meaning have 'mongst those in accord full
"O'er that which cannot be and Liberty endure;—
"They, o'er early native shrines, to heart of Patriot dear, unmoved,—
"Tow'rd land's traditions cold with blood no more a-thrill
"O'er thought and scenes recall'd of what brave forebears prized;—
"With look askance and slight at saving early bond
"The States that bound as one and raised the aegis high
"Earth's bruis'd and wrack'd to draw e'en as the frighted brood
"To mother-wings that fly when looms the threat of ill.
    "So, view young Nation' fair as yet unstable house

"With sand in mortar mixt that tells where weakness is
"Which mightst with safety hold wert building-plan complete,
"Instead of what to all who contemplate must know,
"That e'en scarce by half is destin'd mansion reared:
"Domain of West the taming process waits,—
"She, who toils and pants high Statehood's gates beyond
"With longing look down that charm'd vista bright
"Which holds the lure that myriads sigh to reach,
"As counting the days till she, mature and staid,
"Mayst there in stature full with noted grown-ups stand,—
"Those dazzling one's in Freedom's panoply
"In unity that held in blaze of Glory's day
"And now with brilliance show in Nation's galaxy.
   "How then the case when this, the Great Domain
"All charted is, partitioned full, and golden hour falls
"And her young hulks from out the clearings come,
"As come the lordly herds that hoof-mark wide her plains,
"With cheeks aglow and eyes that dauntless shine,
"With bold and priv'leged press toward Dom'd and storied goal,
"In stately Halls to loom and match their grave compeers!—
"They to hardy habits born,—stalwart, manly, swart!
"With lions wont to cope, and forest foes akin,—
"Endurance tests all won and spurs of Conquest clean,—
"Who ease and softness scorn and all that languor breeds,—
"To hardships all inured, e'en as wert they of eld—
"The sturdy Spartans brave who dream-like Past illume
"Evolving rig'rous mode that boon of Freedom held—
"So they to Nation's boards that in their vigor come
"From Occidental wastes free as their native air,
"With faces bronzed, and hardened palms and brown,—
"Ne'er touch'd by dole save what own servings won,—
"Wilt they to luxuries lapse and, all transform'd, caress
"The Fetish black that self-endeavor blights!
   "The question itself doth answer and, in substance mark
"High turning-point to come when things that are shall pass
"And great new Epoch dawn, with Nation's eyes full ope'd
"To larger-stirring life, e'en as quaint sleeper waked
"From lengthen'd slumber-spell, so grown his world to find,
"That naught of landmarks are, nor those to him once known.
   "For they, new-come, from wide and open land,

"Of that dominion vast need not new tutelage
"To press the lesson home of Country-love and leal!
"Such, their life, their treasure-house,—Nation one and whole!
"Sacred to them as e'er to old the vestal flame,
"And, when doth come the hour that ruthless hands wouldst tear
"The starry emblem down then West shall rise as one
"To night tremendous wak'd, and forth her manhood pour
"With zeal and fury rous'd to high destructive pitch
"As e'er inflam'd wert those in heat of Holy wars
"When flung the frantic fighters wild to whelm the ranks profane,
"And save what precious was, as inner light revealed.
    "So, Time New shall be,—thro' wrench of hearts and tears,
"Blood-letting much,—wailings o'er broken ties, and griefs,—
"New Day's attendants grim,—his doleful Ushers glimpsed
"Adown the range of years,—Fate's chosen ones afar
"To pace the coming Change, and so make clear the way,—
"With solemn tread, and slow, approaching, as if themselves impressed
"By vast o'erturn and woes, with blessings flanked, it brings!
    "For, know, when clouds have cleared and shown the wreckage bare
"And Nature mild, balm-laden, o'er chastened land doth haste
"The gaping wounds to heal and hearts to reconcile,
"With new effulgence then Columbia's sun shall glow
"And vast relief shall be to what wast long repressed,
"And shackled Progress, freed, shalt pass by leaps and bounds
"Those barriers that so held and madst her Prison-house,
"Whilst land throughout shall know and view with eyes alight
"The vim and virile force in Nation's life infused
"By those from Wide Prairie come at Statehood's high behest,
"Whose treasure-house, unlock'd, doth dazzling wonders show—
"E'en as embargoed goods, long held, when ban forbidden, lifts—
"Whilst sons in lofty Hall in salient parts shall aid
"In Adaptations brisk that vast New Order claims."
    Paused the Seeress now and raising slow her head,
Took note of him who sat e'en as grav'd statue, mute,
In his deep eyes the light of intellect aglow,
Observing which, as one, by other's will compelled,
She once more bent, with droop of eyes, dilate,
And voiced yet more what inner vision was:
    "That Query then, in Wisdom's work-shop wrought
"By tools in lap of whirlwind shaped, offspring of hurricane,

"And of all else that things uproot not of stability,
"Which, Proteous-like mayst varied baffling forms assume
"Destructiveness to bring to all inimical
"To weal of country lov'd, to Freedom consecrate,—
"The wedge destined to rive and lay dread Upas tree,
"Nigh half the land that blights, with menace rank, to all—
"View first, of varied roles its subtle force partakes
"In form e'en full equipped as daring horseman swift,
"Booted, spurr'd and grim, impatient steed astride ·
"On all-important quest with writ pursuivant
"With duty charg'd full strict to run Offender down
"And once come with and check'd and duly brought to Earth
"Him, sans ceremony, thence, of garish trappings strip,
"Howe'er pretentious they, or e'en assumptious he,
"Abating naught of zeal since summary way hath leave
"From source exceeding all, mandate of people free,—
"By Freedom's Champion launched at Freemen's stern behest—
"Than more than King's decree, import and weight in sum,—
"Thro' Franchise-right supreme, the sovereign power high,
"Design and purport here in potent voice acclaimed;—
"And once in hand the wretch and Captor's clutch to feel
"Straight rend'ring from him wring, wherein doth warrant lie
"For him and his, e'en as they, Attilian hordes of old,
"To Kansan soil invade with sword, blood-let and flame,
"And homes and lives destroy in ruthless savag'ry
"With civil war in truth in young Dominion waged.
    "Is it from him of feeble palsied hand
"In Ruler's chair who sits all dazed and impotent
"And sees great Ship, to him entrust, toward sure destruction veer,
"With trait'rous crew in glee, own safety-planks secure,
"Gloating o'er salvage rich, which pleasing Fancy shows,
"Of that by others own'd, of steadfast loyalty,—
"The Patriotic-true wide Nation's bounds throughout!—
"He, senile Helmsman weak who there in bitterness
"The bread may fitly eat of sed'lous panderings
"To claims of Cult preposterous, that finds own instrument
"For act and purpose base since Party Shibboleth
"Doth bring gray head to bow and so to utmost yield.
    "E'en thus 'twill be thro' years of instigated strife,
"On fertile Western fields ere greater, wider strife to come,

"Thro' sick'ning Seasons' rounds,—a drab monotony
"Of clashings, killings, burnings—imported outlawry,
"By gold of slave-lords bought, e'en there pour'd lavishly
"Since great the prize outheld—a vast domain and rich
" 'Yond all compare,—a treasure-land to be,
"Than fruitful Nile's deep soil more deep and fertile this;        [view,—
"With Egypt's area fam'd, as Kitchen-patch to Empire's expanse
"A princely realm superb, from whate'er angle seen;
"By lordly rivers flush'd, glad earth to bless and cheer
"And mineral hoards unreck'd in low, land-dotted hills,
"Earth-stores for Thrift to claim when falls the season due,—
"A Wonder-house of wealth 'neath rock and sand-bed hid
"Whence oil shall gush and carbons rise and varied metals, bright,
"As lure to Commerce brisk, her ears afar to hail.
    "Yet, o'er worth of all in run of years to be
"Shall fruits of Tillage show, world-hunger's cries to still
"As myriad workers swarm, as bees in humming hives,
"O'er countless groaning fields, of bounds there limitless—
"To eye's unaided sweep, where'er may vision turn,—
"The bount'ous crops to reap 'neath monster threshers' roar
"And o'er wide earth forth send where stalks e'er craving need;—
" 'Garden of West' as known by waning Tribesmen red
"Thro' long tradition taught that favor'd wast their race
"By Spirit-Guardian high, their lives to there implant
"Where ground such plenty brings and streams so gen'rous yield.
    "Comes then new sort in range of imagery
"That Nature discrim'nate culls in spacious garden-plot
"Of varied humans, whose eyes likewise dilate        ·
"O'er what thro' ages long red brother knew and prized
"And, him ousting and forcing on,—no more to reckon with
"They in twain factions break ingloriously and strive
"The favor'd land to win,—one long and wild melee
"Each 'gainst other warring, in spleen and hatred keen
"As if one flag and Nation sole, didst not the fealty claim
"Of them and those close rang'd,—an omen sinister,
"For, wast it not enough, owners—rightful—dispossessed
"Shouldst old homes depart, and, as helpless nomads go
"That they, new-come, might enter peacefully and take
"Instead of warrings wild 'gainst own blood and creed,—
"Such pillage, burnings, plunderings as wouldst ever shame

"Those hapless ones, hight Savages, who sorrowfully pass,
"Their faces turned toward slanting rays, with swift suggestion grim
" 'Tis typical of what their day and kind awaits,
"E'en as other scene, of those, as Civilized appraised,
"Is symptomatic quite of what for them grim future bodes,—
"Two wrongs, thus sown, to rise and spread their noxious seed,   [claim."
" 'Till fateful crops upspring which shall more than sweat of reapers
    Here paused the dame with change of pose and quick uplift
Of head there droop'd and eyes of introspective cast
That scarce didst hearer's presence sense, from inner vision's show,
Whilst in reverie deep she for a space did rest
In such spell of calm profound as madst there eloquent
The silence tense, a scenic break and weird,
In which didst onward throng a host of images,
On airy Fancy's film, in stately pageantry,
Of what had Seeress limn'd,—the spacious Kansan fields—
The smoke and flames of strife—the hapless Settler's woe
As brave defenders rous'd with weapons nondescript;—
The wild Missourian hordes o'er turgid stream that swarm—
The onset and overturn of peace and order fair,—
The rooting up and laying waste in barb'rous riotry,
Of vine and tree and rude home-shelter, dear,
'Yond let of Code or rule of war,—the acts of wantoness,
Which naught in breast of man but vicious Cult couldst breed;—
Prostrating forms of Law,—throttling electorate
Where'er collect wert members seen, from home and workshop drawn,
As such, to duty high perform, when,—lo! to mockery
By lawless onslaught changed, and still must Kansas writhe
'Neath cloud of doubt so rais'd to make e'en debatable
Prepost'rous tale that major vote doth black Engraft approve.
    All these and more did pass and then inclining, she
With eyes half-closed the thread of theme resumed:
    "The Western Ophir fair, too rich for hope of peace
"In young and ardent years howe'er may yearnings be,
"Shall raging nightmares breed in peaceful settler's sleep,
"And so to those of Nation wide,—e'en worse in Council high
"At land's impressive Seat, contending Statesmen 'twixt;—
"The salt on Friction's smart,—the foe to wonted poise
"Of those who erst were calm,—Deportment's broken staff—
"Discord's apple—Dudgeon's spur—fierce Contention's bone;—

"A shuttlecock e'er constant knock'd, as high all passions swell;
"Theme explosive e'er, with acrimony charged
"And all else that choler knows;—e'er cause of Order's breach
"Wherein high names show low; e'en Code of Courtesy
"And set Decorum prim, vacating, leaving unadorned
"The stately Homes of Form, and Incubations sage
"Of Statute-Laws, and Measures varied and numerous
"For weal of land at large,—now scenes of travesty,—
"With gory pen of bulls comparing,—place of collisions sharp,—
"Of deadly challenge—assaults—the brutal bludgeon-blow,—
"An interregnum grim, of wild, ebulliating blood
"O'er Kansan broils brought on, she of woes innumerable,
"Who, 'gainst barr'd doors shalt knock for that admission just
"Which Stateshood's rights do claim, e'er sharp rebuff to meet
"Since dominant are those who wouldst her spirit tame
"And so, perforce alliance make that untold prestige means
"To Pact of Party great and black accompaniment,—
"To weal of florid Clime an acquisition vast,
"Present bounds enlarging, strengthing great the arm
"E'en long oppressive felt, from testy Cult that sways
"And wouldst the Roast e'er rule where'er might feasting be,—
"Menace of days to Peace the bounds of land throughout.
    "So 'tis to be 'till mental forge in stressful, fateful hour
"Shalt verbal weapon shape, fine as the proverb'd mill
"The grist of gods that grinds with patience infinite
"Thro' years of wrongs uncurb'd, by Retribution fed
"Men's evil deeds to sift and so to judgment bring,
"And punishment thence mete proportioned to the ill
"All in the destin'd time whate'er mayst be the lapse,—
"The inveitable that comes,—the rend'ring adequate.
    "And foreordained it is that reckn'ing here shall be
"For some dark things of past that Horror's chill doth know,—
"That cheeks hast brought to blush as shiv'ring dread did strike
"And shame, that such shouldst be, e'en there by stately Dome
" 'Neath which, e'en all misplaced, shows Liberty content,
"Sweet boon in effigy, to symbolize what Patriot-blood hadst won,
"Which, wert she endow'd, 'midst other trappings there, with ears
"That mystically full sentient were, and sharp,
"Might hear the Crier's voice in raucous outpour raised
"In Auction yard hard by, 'midst jeers and jestings coarse,

"As he doth high dilate on living wares he sells,
"Partic'larizing close, as bared and dull stand they
"In form of man or woman, or shrinking, lisping child,
"Or lad, or maid half-grown, penn'd so like sheep or swine.     [dowered
    "Such things of blight shall West e'er know,—the land so richly
"By Him that Mercy is,—shall there such scenes e'er be?
" 'Tis not so writ on face of stalwart manhood true          [herself
"That fair New England knows, nor Middle-land nor rising West,
"Howe'er may threats and bluster be, and Kansan thatch-roofs burn,
"Or brave defenders fall.  Hark! the mill doth rumble low
"As if its grind, well on, did sense some mystic tie
"Deep to its purpose held, and occult greeting give,
"For it doth use, in its Fulfillments great,
"Varied strange instruments, as if in training-school its own
"Wert those enrolled for purpose high who all in season ripe
"Shalt forth emerge, earth-thrilling Change to bring,
"Arousing wonderment wide-spread and wrongly deem'd phenomenal,
"As if 'twere Nature's way to in spasmodics work
"And suddenly outflare, some world-arresting thing to do,
"As Hindoo fakir lithe, who makes the plant to rise
"From seed to growth mature, whilst daz'd onlookers view;
"Instead of what is truth that she in slowness plods,
"Moving by changeless laws thro' generations long—
"By men computed so—e'er weaving fabric sure
"With no ungathered threads in mesh of purpose fine
"All by her deft hand caught and wrought with certitude
"Thro' countless intricacies, the ply invisible;
"Wide universe her field, the Fates her ministers,
"As subtle web she weaves for fixt eventful hour
"When Time full ripeness shows and,—the task complete!
"Beheld the toppling thrones and mighty monarchs flung
"Low as the dust where beggar wails, and, transformation view!—
"The altered state of Majesty that yesterday didst reign
"With pomp that e'er attends and gaze of millions awed!
"Brought now to reck'ning swift with house and kindred-kind!—
"They, who from common ills wert ever deemed immune!—
"Of dazzling raiment stript and taught ungently to obey,
"Where erst commanded they, as so that regal line,
"Whose sins, long moulting, wingeth thus to home,
"The dazed Descended so to plague in this, the reck'ning hour;—

"Now bow'd with woes, e'en by own servants scorned,
"And haled with gibe and jeer to dreary region far
"Where winter's rigors gnaw and erst sad exile moaned,
"For trump'd offense full guiltless of, on perjured tongues condemned,
"And pined his life away because same princely hand
"Hadst so decreed, with naught of Mercy shown
"When worldly state swell'd high and will of his wast law!—
"He here same anguish now to know and tenfold horrors more
"From those, long cent'ries, score who bring of wrongs unspeakable
"Him and his against, and holdst the bitter cup
"Which he, and those most dear, unto the dregs must drink
"Ere cometh sum of all, the culminating act,—
"The expiation cum'lative that cancels debt long held
" 'Gainst him and those before,—in one red welter paid!"


*   *   *


As ceas'd the dame a silence, awesome, weird
On rounding space did fall and leave the hearing wracked
And straining yet for sound of that which now was mute
Yet ling'ring ghostlike still on ear-drums tense to beat,
Res'nant, vibrant spell of volum'd noise, as seemed
As deep-mouth'd shell convolvulate the sea that simulates
With e'er continuous roar as breakers 'gainst a beach
And howling winds, withal that rise and fall in turn
As tho' in unison from crested swell to ocean-trough;—
A fearsome void profound with phantom chorus-scream
That holds the senses still'd; or as Aeolean strings
Far inner chords that search and transport hearer back
To days long gone and scenes which, resurrected, live
As thick throng mem'ries old and render Present null;
Or e'en as break abysmal, sheer, some landscape fair that marks
And holds one stock and daz'd as yawning depths there show
Whilst swift doth ope the mind to drear imaginings
In clutch of Terrors troop of things impalpable
In eeyrie shapes that flit from Superstition's brew
E'er in wait that lie to goodly sense o'erawe
And fain wouldst captive make wert not sane self alert
To interpose full sharp and bid vile brood decamp.

And she, the Seeress swart, with lips unmoving sat
In contemplation fixt, in her dark eyes a flame
That all consuming seemed, the beacon-light of that
By inner vision glimps'd, the faint and storm-girt shore
Toward which full set wast Nation's ship, by treach'rous pilots steered,
Whilst he, late hearer held, as one transfix'd and dumb
Until, at length a stir, that tension'd spell absolved
As she, to theme last touch'd recurring, darkly summarized:
    "Thus Reparation comes oft in appalling way
"Proportion'd full to scope of long persisting ills
"In pace with high Abuse that rides the road ahead,
"The faint-glimps'd Trailers grim from Land of Nemesis,
"Oft shadowy and vague but e'er untiring set
"Ne'er ceasing onward press,—in zeal relaxing ne'er,
"As hounds unleashed that speed and scent where vision fails
"With deep-mouth'd fearful bay as chase doth shorter grow
"And tho' pursued rides high and seemeth all immune
"In end no diff'rence is save cup of woe enlarged,
"When grim pursuit is o'er and comes the reck'ning drear.
    "So shalt blood-flow exact—from groaning bondsman drawn,—
"And ev'ry lash-welt rais'd on quiv'ring flesh unspared
"Ten times ten-fold its toll shall Masters' blood requite
"Till hecatombs shall fall and drench the soil, erst red
"From stain of writhing forms that mark'd the Helots' woe,
"Whilst pillar'd homes of note in stately view that loomed
"A prey to flames shall be o'er land of Bondage wide
"And all the Pharaon ills on Egypt's clime that fell
"For wrongs to Hebrews done, e'en less in sum shall show
"Than those slow-marshaling now 'neath Retribution's eye,
"Thro' dust of time to grow in gathered strength and might
"Till he, of mother born upon this date, in fine,
"A generation's space shall not in years o'errun
"Ere come and gone on mission set those dread ministers,—
"Avengers stern of hid'ous wrongs, their work in full compassed
"Leaving in wake of them what tongue would fain not tell,—
"The wreck of towns and cities fair, and devastation wide
"O'er goodly lands that were when wealth and prestige high
"Wert told and sung,—o'er width of world declaimed
"And scenes rose-hued didst rise, and princely pageantries

"Didst Beauty's eyes dilate, and noble manly trials
"At Fair and Tournament did captivate and thrill;—
"Feats of skill and venture bold, with dim traditions linked
"Of Old World's Past, Romance and Chivalry,
"In Sunny clime redivivus,—all, all to pass and leave
"The waste of field and grove and grand ancestral seat,
"Relic of days, baronial-blent when wast in lordly sway
"High-living and its pomps, when lavish hands didst spread
"The fruits of unrequited toil, and Master of Manor rich
"With landed prototype o'er wide seas didst vie
"In pillared massy pile on verdant shore or eminence
"Wherefrom mirth and music rose as lightsome hours flew
"On wings of joy and transports gay, of sweet delights and bliss,—
"Merriment unbounded, free, to Southland-clime distinct;—
"Racy and riotous, unsparing of the nightly hour,
"Doom'd—ah! too soon to end in black and gaping walls
"With scarce a vestige left of splendors, once the theme
"Of wonder wide whereon didst eyes of stranger dwell
"In admiration vast,—in ruins all in future near, to be!
"With grim Decay at ev'ry turn,—a scarr'd and barren land,
"With unfed earth infertile grown, and they who once didst lord—
"Master, man-drivers all,—the battle trench to fill and leave
"Once happy mates and children fair, to know the bitterness
"Of blighting Change that maketh joy a memory."
   With pause abrupt she who had so steadfast held
Attention tense of him, erect now sat and gazed
Upon him full, in her deep eyes a look
Of strain and weariness which he, observing, moved
From posture set his frame, lank sinewy, and rose,—
Act scarce conscious,—with face abstracted, grave,
That showed a mind borne far, as one from dream awaked
With vision dim and blurr'd and varied ponderings
O'er semblances and threads disjoined,—in dark bewilderment;—
A mind 'yond wont perplext, confus'd, o'erwrought;
With bounds and bearings vague, and futile gropings, strange,
Familiar hold to find and normal poise regain,
Which, compass'd at length, he, mindful of her due,
His thanks didst voice and well-meant tribute pay
For that disclosed which so hadst interest held.

But she, ignoring praise with shaking head and look
Of gravity full marked, and voice intoning deep:
"Too long your patience good, I fear was strained
"Yet belief doth justify, and I have sought and yet shall seek
"Revealment full to make of that in wait which lies
"Brewing its large brew for Nation's lips to quaff,
"That you may wiser be to act the mighty part
"To you alone assign'd in due appointed hour
"When Country's need swells large and naught but Superman
"Can save the stricken one,—a man intuitive,
"Of courage blent with faith,—patience infinite,
"And spirit that ne'er flags howe'er may body weary be;—
"Of mind that keeps its poise when others round it sink
"In sheer dismay and fear, and wouldst wild panic breed;—
"Such, he must be in Nation's dire extremity;—
"E'en more than Patriot,—a lover of his kind
"Who, for stricken feel from depth of heart compassionate,
"And o'er griefs of others mourns;—a pillow primed with thorns
"On which his head must lie through stressful spell of years
"Of ne'er-relaxing zeal in purpose fixt,—his land belov'd to save.
"So, if you who have so honored me shall hence go impressed
"That truth to you was shown—e'er if in part you believe,—
"It is enough and more, to place on me the debt
"That Gratitude doth owe, and make me debtor still
"If on the morrow, as time may suit, or on the after day—
"Either or both—and days thereafter, until all is bared
"You wilt come and hear; for this, your horoscope,
"Is that of Country, too, in coming strenuous time;
"So may it well be said that in land's travail and woe,
"When you so much shall be, your fortunes merge as one,
"Since devotion deep and effort constant, ceaselessly
"On part of you to save your natal soil, in stress,
"Doth blend your names inseparably, making in sense synonymous
"The two, howe'er may variation be
"In term of designation of the clime itself.
"What hidden yet remains behind the drape of years
"That, you shall know, e'en as the weaver knows his woof;
"For busy the hands of Destiny
"That course of Nations mark, e'en as that of mortal man,

"And move full swift, anon, factors in the great upswell
"That country nigh shall strain unto the breaking point,—
"The gath'ring forces glimps'd at ev'ry turn that show,
"All must'ring for the hour when great Displacement comes,
"E'en as a rock,—as fam'd Gibraltar, huge—
"From source invisible upsprung, the ocean's breast to vex,
"This Thing shall fall and vast commotion bring,
"Drawing eyes of world amaz'd,—in strained excitement tense—
"O'er upstir, and din in land e'en late as Model held,—
"So much of Change to come, and all in time so brief,—
"If from gladsome birth-date reck'd,—Change, so stupendous, great,
"As makes a Nation old e'en tho' in years yet young!—
"E'en more of drastic shift, bloodlet and sacrifice
"Than e'er red page of Europe's civil broils have shown,
"From War of Roses vain to drab Cromwellian days;—
"Or e'en to gasping France when deep in throes wast she
"And wrack'd Parisian streets didst run in crimson streams,
"And shapely necks wert bared to steel of guillotine,
"To bring solution strange onlooking world to daze,
"E'en as shalt tumult here a vital Problem solve—
"That round ·the Nation's neck hath as a milestone hung.
    "So light of Hope on thee is fixt, and thro' the years shall be
"Unto thy kind a boon to make the spirits glad,
"Where else hearts would be low o'er deep incertitude,
"From land's turmoil upsprung, and wanton waste of blood,
"As noble heads sink down in battle's wild acclaim;—
"Ye the rock, round with the raging storm shall beat
"And angry breakers lash, with spumes and swirls of spray,
"With naught defin'd and clear in dreary prospect shown
"Save stalwart form of thee at troubled Nation's helm
"With grasp held tense and firm and lips compress'd and set
"And Resolution grim in face and poise exprest,
"As if thine eyes didst glimpse what wast from others hid,—
"The dawn of brighter days beyond the rim of gloom
"And storm-wrack'd ship in port, its 'perilled voyage o'er,
"And ye, the Captain worn, relaxt in rest and peace."

www.ingramcontent.com/pod-product-compliance
Lightning Source LLC
Chambersburg PA
CBHW022143020726
47496CB00008B/2539